Witches Seduction

Mandy's Story

The Double Winker's Club Series

Laura J. Kendall

Witches Seduction (The Double Winker's Club Series Book 2)
Copyright 2013

Dedication

To my soul mate   may our paths entwine during this lifetime ~

Acknowledgements

Thank you to my friend and real life medevac pilot who did his best to help me with the crash scene. All errors in technique are purely mine. Face it you are much smarter than I and frankly I know I didn't get it as right on as you instructed.

For my facebook and real life friends (Debbie E, Mike F, Arlene R) who helped me discover character names, places and plot I thank you! If I left anyone out please email me!

My readers you are the most awesome group of people I've ever had the pleasure to write for and if I'm lucky - meet in person. Thank you for supporting me!

To my real life Greyhound daughters - Kelsey, Queenie and Kit Kat - I love you and thank you for rescuing me.

To all who still believe in magic I am happy to be among you.

ONE

August 1st

"Holy hell, is this really happening?" Mandy Devine shook her head as she looked into her side mirror and gunned the engine of her white SL 550 Mercedes Roadster, merging onto the highway.

The day had started out with heavy thunderstorms which had fit in perfectly with her mood. This was eve of her, "turning a half century old," milestone birthday. She'd always been the pretty one. The Barbie doll look alike—now she felt like Barbie's grandmother.

She blinked through the glare as the sun finally peaked through the storm clouds. She pulled out mirrored aviator sunglasses from her purse and slipped them on. She then pushed the button that lowered the roof of the powerful convertible. The warm wind blew through her waist length blonde hair which was heavily streaked with brown highlights. Never in a million years, would the motorist she just shot past, dream the beautiful woman inside the hot sports car was seriously depressed.

The divorce from her billionaire ex-husband, William Devine was finally over. He'd gotten the mansion he'd wanted ever since they'd separated and she now lived with her best friend and fellow witch-paramedic, Kit Montaque.

Her life couldn't get much more depressing. No home, no boyfriend, and turning fifty years old tomorrow. Her friends Kit, Connie, Kandy and Niki, all thought she needed to find a hot young stud and get laid. Yeah right. She glanced into the rear view mirror and frowned seeing those fine lines around her eyes. She didn't believe a stud was going to find her attractive enough anymore to get laid.

Stomping on the gas in frustration, she floored the Roadster without thinking about the speed. Nothing mattered, except out running the ugly thoughts in her head. Through the red haze of annoyance in her mind, Mandy heard a siren and glanced down at the speedometer. Eyes wide, she couldn't believe it read 100 miles per hour. She eased off the pedal and coasted over to the shoulder. Why even try and pretend the siren wasn't for her?

Red and blue flashing strobe lights filled her rearview mirror as she placed her hands on the steering wheel so as not to spook the trooper. She watched him get out of the cruiser with a frown on his face, so deep it nearly reached his toes.

"Damn it, could this day get any worse?" she muttered as she heard his boots crushing the gravel on approach. She took a deep breath and looked up into the very unhappy trooper's face.

"Do you know why I stopped you miss?" He stood inches from her car with his hand resting on his gun. He glanced down at her inspection sticker and then at the paramedic sticker above it. Disbelief covered his handsome face as he shook his head. "You're a paramedic?" he said with undisguised sarcasm.

Her worry turned to anger as the trooper walked around the Mercedes inspecting it from stem to stern. Her eyes narrowed behind the mirrored aviators.

"That's what the sticker says, so it must be true." She nodded her head, her sarcasm matching his. "May I reach into my purse for my license, registration and insurance card, Officer?"

"With that attitude, you must be a medic." His mouth twitched from trying to suppress a smile.

She handed him her information, rolling her eyes. He took it and walked back to his cruiser without another word. She watched as he picked up the radio mic and called in her information. "Call Kit," she said out loud. The Mercedes dialed the number.

Kit answered first ring. "Hello Mandy, how's the birthday girl?"

"About to get a ticket for going a hundred miles per hour on Route 287," Mandy sighed. "If I was still young and hot I'd have no problem talking my way out of it. The trooper is sexy as hell too; I'd say he's a cross between the cops from Adam 12 and Chips. Did I mention he's young and hot? Damn, why couldn't I stay young? Surely there must be a spell..."

"Yo Sista, stop picking on yourself!" Kit said sharply, breaking Mandy's self-disparaging rant before it even started. "Stop beating yourself up this minute! You're an amazing and beautiful woman and there's not a hot, young trooper with a pair of eyes and a brain in his, pardon the pun—head that would write a ticket to a medic."

"Notice, you didn't say, he won't write me a ticket because I am a hot, beautiful blonde medic." Mandy huffed loudly. "I hate my life! I have no home, no man and no more looks! Oh hell, here he comes, gotta go." She ended the call with a quick goodbye. She shook her head, sighing loudly just as the trooper stopped next to her door.

"Having a bad day Mrs. Devine?" He handed back her license and other papers.

"You could say that." She looked up at the handsome young stud and nodded. "Please just give me my ticket and let me continue on with my miserable day."

His mouth formed a beautiful smile. "Now what kind of fellow emergency provider would I be, if I ticketed a beautiful, blonde, paramedic on her birthday?"

Mandy lowered her sunglasses to get a better look at the expression on the trooper's face. He seemed sincere, although she doubted the beautiful blonde part. She smiled back at him and laughed sadly. "Well trooper, thanks for the pity pardon, I appreciate it."

His gaze seemed to penetrate her glasses and lock onto her blue eyes. "Oh, I assure you Mrs. Devine, there is no pity on my part," he told her in a sexy voice.

"It's Ms. by the way." Mandy wiggled in her seat, pulling down the short jean skirt she'd worn.

"I'm sorry?" He shook his head. "Ms.?"

"Not Mrs. Devine, Ms. Devine. I just finished getting the big D." It felt good saying it out loud for the first time to someone other than her friends.

He laughed deeply. It was one of those laughs that sounded wonderful to her wounded spirit and she found herself laughing too, for the first time in months.

"Where are you off to on this stormy day?" He glanced up at the swirling dark clouds bearing down on them. He motioned towards the button on the dash. "You'd better put your top back on if you don't want to get wet."

She lowered her aviators down her nose and squinted up at the sexy trooper. "Yeah wouldn't want to get wet... not with my top off."

His face burned a deep red as he got her innuendo. "Oh no... not what I meant... I really mean the storms coming on pretty quickly and you..."

She giggled and winked. "Got ya. I'm just having a little fun with you, troop." Holy smokes she was actually flirting with a guy who was probably young enough to be her son. "Thanks again for not giving an old lady a ticket on her birthday."

"Honey, if you're an old lady, sign me up for the nursing home." He hesitated for a minute then continued. "I'd love to see you again sometime."

A sharp clap of thunder boomed as rain drops began to fall breaking the moment in two. As if shaking himself out of a spell the trooper tapped her door and pointed to the button. "Get that roof up before you get drenched. Have a wonderful birthday Ms. Devine." With that he was gone.

She pushed the button and sighed as the roof went up and over her head. "Oh well, so much for that." She smiled, a little amazed that her good mood was still with her despite the abrupt break off of the almost being asked out on a date speech.

Easing the Mercedes back onto the roadway, she watched her hot young stud get smaller and smaller in her rearview mirror.

TWO

Trooper Therron (Jessie) Reyes-Mythos got back into his cruiser just as the skies opened up. The rain tapped loudly on the roof as he ran his hands through his chestnut brown hair, styled in the popular cop crew-cut.

His senses were on high alert as he picked up the mic and notified dispatch that he was secure from the stop. Could it really be, after all this time? All the signs pointed to a big fat yes! What a big dope! He'd been about to ask her out and that stupid clap of thunder had suddenly made him a big chicken shit.

He looked down at the bulge that was still apparent in his pants; his reaction to Ms. Devine was causing a bit of discomfort. He knew without a shadow of a doubt what he'd see when he reached up and angled the rear view mirror. Glowing amber eyes glared back at him and a shiver ran down his spine.

When he'd been standing by her car, he'd felt the warmth rushing to his cock and knew his eyes were reflecting his confusion as that secreted part of his brain opened once again. Unfortunately, the damn rain had come, disrupting his composure and shattering the moment.

There had been no recognition of him on her part and it cut him to the core. His one love for all time had been inches from him, and she'd had no clue who he was.

He licked his lips and ran his tongue over his teeth, the sharpness of his incisors filling him with desire. His witch was back and he had found her again and there was nothing and no one that was going to stop him from claiming her as his own once more. She was his and he was going to make sure she remembered.

He switched off the emergency lights and as soon as there was an opening in the line of traffic, he accelerated smoothly onto the highway. He frowned when he remembered Mandy's expression of disbelief at his simple compliment to her. Didn't she realize that she was the most beautiful woman on this earth?

Even two hundred years hadn't dimmed his desire for her; she was everything to him and always would be. Looking upward, he silently thanked, OM, creator of all beings—human, vampire, witch, weres' and all other creatures in the universe.

He had been born Therron Reyes-Mythos and was both hunter and healer of the Adulane Vampire Race. He was the son of Zacharias Mythos, one of the most powerful of all vampires, and was also half human witch, thanks to his Mom, Raven Reyes, High Priestess of the Santigo Coven. Sadly, she hadn't survived in her human form, thanks to the witch hunts in the 1600. He smiled thinking of her back home pacing back and forth on the windowsill, enjoying the sun's rays, in her current incarnation.

He wasn't well liked by any of the other troopers, not that he blamed them. Face it, he'd been labeled a freak ever since Trooper Larry Powers had pulled up on a wreck and spotted him in the middle of a healing. Of course, the asshole had no idea what was going on as the lights from his troop car had lit up the night, illuminating the darkness exposing the fact that he was kneeling next to a wrecked car, letting the driver suckle from his wrist.

Therron pushed the thoughts of his status with his fellow troopers out of his mind and turned back to the woman he'd just let drive away. He wasn't going to let her go that easily. He remembered her address, so he knew damn well she was coming back this way in order to go home and he'd be waiting.

Approaching the next exit he decided to exit off and get something to eat. He never hunted on an empty stomach and this prize was going to suck all the life out of him by the end of the night. At least that was his plan; he sure hoped it worked out the way he wanted.

THREE

Mandy's heart pounded and she fought to catch her breath. In the shadows of her mind, the memory of the trooper's amber eyes came back to her. She was convinced that he had been able to see everything that was hidden within her. She' hadn't felt so alive in years.

The name plate on his powerful chest had read - Trooper Reyes-Mythos, which meant he was half Greek and half Spanish, a very potent combination, especially in a hot blooded male. He'd actually been flirting with her and her with him.

Her mood lifted and suddenly she felt like the sexiest woman on the face of God's green earth, until once again she felt doubt crowding in.

"Geez girl get a grip! The guy was young and he clearly knows what an old broad you are after wishing you a happy birthday." She gripped the wheel tightly, and for what felt like the hundredth time, checked to see if a troop car was behind her. When she was younger, there wouldn't have been a second of doubt on that score, because back then, they always wanted her. Now nobody did.

She signaled and got off the exit for New Hope. Luckily, she found parking on the street but she waited a few minutes for the rain to stop.

The sun was beginning to win the battle for the sky, as the dark clouds moved off into the distance.

Opening the door she eased out of the Mercedes and headed down the cobblestone street to her favorite store, The Goddess Crone. A bell jingled as she pulled open the glass door that had a witch riding a broom etched on it.

Inhaling deeply, Mandy let the scent of the candles and herbs fill her senses, and calm her spirit. Aisles and aisles of other worldly goodies filled the store which is one of the reason she loved coming here so much. She picked up a black shopping basket as she smiled at the owner, Lady Rorry Maveen.

"Hello Mandy," Rorry said, cheerfully.

"Hi Lady Maveen, how are you?" Mandy rested her basket on the frosted glass countertop. "It feels like forever since I've been to your beautiful shop."

"Exactly six months." She tapped her temple. "I never forget my favorite customers." She ran her fingers through her thick shoulder length black hair that was streaked with a dark blue hue.

Mandy smiled. "Why thank you, Lady Maveen, I have always thought of you as my mentor."

"Are you looking for anything specific today?" Lady Maveen's deep brown eyes locked onto Mandy's blue ones and smiled. "Your aura is different than last time you were here. It's light and happy. Did something happen?"

Mandy blushed. "I just got pulled over by the sexiest state trooper I've ever seen. He actually flirted with me, and I don't know, for some reason I feel giddy, yet at the same time depressed." She grimaced, while shaking her head. "It's strange getting old, Rorry, I'm turning a half a century old at midnight and I feel it."

Lady Maven walked out from behind the counter and wrapped Mandy in a great big bear hug. "It doesn't have to be that way, Honey." She motioned for Mandy to follow her through a door labeled private.

Mandy didn't hesitate. Lady Rorry Maven was a powerful witch and true friend. If anyone could help her feel better about turning the big five-O, she could.

Three white candles illuminated an otherwise dark room while soft mystical music played in the background. In the middle of the room sat an ornate chair decorated with jewels that had powerful affirmations carved in the hard wood.

Lady Maveen waved Mandy to the chair and to place her purse on a small white table.

Mandy watched as The Lady went to work, mixing up a spell filled with ingredients that she claimed would reignite Mandy's life's passions, that had been missing for so long from her life.

"Mandy sat back in the chair." There's a button on the side there," The Lady pointed out, "Yes, that's it, the chair reclines, and I'd like you to be in a meditative state when I do the spell. In a moment or two a beautiful Goddess meditation will start playing on the system. It is guided by High Priestess Sapphire Moon, an amazing woman and teacher. Let her words guide you as you slowly begin to let go of this world, and move into the other.

In complete trust, Mandy closed her eyes and lay back, surrendering herself to the Goddess meditation.

Facing north, Rorry stood at the Wiccan altar preparing the spell. When she was ready, she transitioned the meditation to soft new age music.

"I'm going to begin Mandy. This is a special spell I have crafted specifically for you. I believe it will be just what you need to get your mojo back and start enjoying the life you are meant to be living. Please open your eyes when you are ready and join me at the altar."

Mandy opened her eyes and stretched, feeling ready for the spell that was coming her way. She lifted herself out of the chair and walked to the altar.

Rorry waited, dressed in a deep blue velvet floor length witches cape with a hood. "Please stand here." She indicated a specific spot before the beautiful altar. "You will be facing north for the majority of the spell, although we will be honoring each direction during the incantations."

Mandy stood silently before the altar which was filled with everything Rorry needed for the spell. She glanced around the medium sized room. The white candles which glowed with sparkly light were set out in such a way so they would form a circle around the altar and the area where the spell work was being done.

Rorry held out a rose quartz wand that sparkled with inlaid diamonds and other glittering jewels. She pointed it towards the edge of the circle. "I invoke our guardian elements of fire, water, air and earth to form a circle of protection. Keep us safe within this protected area and keep all evil entities out. She rang an ornate bell invoking the universal powers.

Mandy, already a well learned and respected witch in her own right, watched the High Priestess at work. Every time she was in the presence of Lady Maveen, she always learned something new.

"I've gathered three candles. Each symbolizes reinvention and new phases in your life, Mandy. To make this spell have a lasting effect I'll need you to participate with me."

Mandy nodded. "I'd love to. Thank you for doing this for me."

Rorry pointed to three round candles, each twelve inches in height. One pink, one red and one purple. "Please pick up the red candle and the patchouli oil next to it."

Mandy held the candle and oil.

"Coat the red candle from end to wick with the patchouli oil and place it in the crystal holder when you are done. Next, take the pink candle and coat it with rose oil from end to wick. Finally take the purple candle and coat it with frankincense oil from end to wick."

Mandy coated each candle as instructed and then carefully set them in their holders. The heavenly fragrances filled her senses and relaxed her further into the moment.

"Now take the rose quartz and rinse it in salt water to cleanse all negative charges and energy." Lady Maveen indicated a beautiful pink crystal. "Dry it with this cloth and set it beside the pink candle." She handed Mandy a soft clean purple cloth.

After cleansing the rose quartz and drying it, Mandy set it down on the altar and watched Lady Maveen light a long white candle. She walked over and stood beside Mandy.

"I've sensed for a long while now that you had lost an essential part of yourself, Mandy. Your sensual, sexy, self-confident and feminine self."

"Yes, since menopause, I just feel old and about as attractive as a rock." Mandy exhaled softly. "I'd give anything to be young and feel good about myself and life again."

Lady Maveen smiled. "Your body will be the age it is, but your soul is ageless. The spell we are doing today is for the soul and I promise you that when you leave here you will have your sexy back."

Mandy giggled. "Lady Maveen, I've never heard you talk like this before!"

Lady Maveen laughed, then began giving instructions for the spell. "As I say the spell, I want you to echo it back as you light each candle. Shall we begin?"

"I'm ready." Mandy smiled as she gripped the long white candle already burning brightly.

"I'll tell you when to begin your part, Mandy. Let us center ourselves for a few minutes as you envision what it is you want for your ideal life; in your relationships with a lover, your friends and what you want yourself to look like. What you believe, you shall receive."

The two women stood in silence for several minutes, each lost in their own world of thoughts. Lady Maveen broke the silence.

"Let's get your sexy back. This spell we are about to begin is designed to make you see what an amazing, beautiful and sexy woman you are, no matter what your age, Mandy. It will open that part of you that you have squashed down with self-doubt and old thinking. It will open you only to men who are attracted to your whole package without the aim to use you as has happened in the past. Open yourself and your mind and know that you have grown into a woman who is powerful enough to hold her own, yet she still willing to allow a man to love her."

Picking up her crystal wand, Lady Maveen held it out in front of her. "We ask you Goddess and God to favor us with your power, protection and love. Mandy, please light the pink candle before you. Pink symbolizes love and friendship with yourself. The rose oil it is coated with enhances your beauty, sexuality and peace within. The rose quartz stone symbolizes your connection to our mother earth."

Using the white candle Mandy touched the wick of the pink candle and watched as it took hold glowing brightly.

"With the lighting of this candle, I empower you to love, to open your heart like a morning dove. You know your power—you own it inside—from this day it will no more hide. Pink is for love and now it is yours. Open your heart—open your mind—let it shine. So mote it be."

Mandy inhaled softly, feeling the power of the words flow through her. "With the lighting of this candle I am empowered to love. To open my heart like a morning dove. I know my power—I own it inside—no more will I hide. Pink is for love, and now it is mine. I open my heart and mind and let my love shine. So mote it be." Mandy opened herself to the power of love rushing back inside her.

Lady Maveen pointed to the red candle. "Red is for sexual passion. The patchouli oil coating it is for lustful desire, animal magnetism and awakening your own sexual desires."

Mandy touched the red candles wick and watched as the flame shot up into the air filling the room with light.

"With the lighting of this candle, I empower you to unleash your raw sensual desires within. Let them roar to the surface no longer denied, so you can now find yourself a man to ride. He will be the one who lets you be you–sensual, sexual, free to explore, a wild woman forever more. Red is for sexual, sexy, wild passion and now it is yours. Open your heart, mind and body and start to explore, this passion is yours forever more. So mote it be."

Mandy swallowed deeply.

"Go on, Sista get your sexy back. It is now or never." Lady Maveen winked.

"With the lighting of this candle, I empower myself to unleash my raw sensual desires. To let them roar to the surface no longer denied, so I can now find myself a man to ride. This man will be one who lets me be me—sexual, sexy, sensual, free, a wild woman evermore to be. Red is for sexual, wild passion, and now it is mine. I open my heart, mind, body and soul and start to explore this passion forever more. So mote it be." Mandy glanced over at Lady Maveen. "I hope you don't mind that I added a few more words of my own."

Lady Maveen smiled brightly. "The more words that resonate with you the more powerful this spell will be."

Lady Maveen pointed to the remaining purple candle. She took the white candle from Mandy and handed her an ornate knife in its stead. "Pick up the purple candle and with the knife, I want you to carve the one word you want to live by. Purple symbolizes power, power that is yours to command."

Mandy picked up the purple candle and without hesitation carved the word FEARLESS on its side. "For too long I have hidden and have been afraid. Today I begin new again and I will live FEARLESSLY to the end. My power is mine to own and command. No one can take it from me, on this I take a stand."

Lady Maveen inhaled deeply. "Well said Mandy, may I take a moment to connect to your words and empower myself? I couldn't have said it any better, for I too, need to take back my life and live it fearlessly."

Mandy nodded and closed her eyes giving Lady Maveen time to embrace the words and their meanings for herself.

"Thank you Mandy, I always learn something new every time I have the opportunity to work with you. I too will embrace living fearlessly." She took back the knife and handed Mandy the burning white candle.

Mandy felt a rush of energy surge through her body as the Goddess connection of strength passed between the two powerful witches. "As do I, Lady Maveen. Together we will support each other in living fearlessly and powerfully." Mandy placed the purple candle, with FEARLESS carved into the wax, back into its deep amethyst crystal holder.

"With the lightening of this candle I empower you to embrace and own your power. To claim it as your own banishing all past powerlessness you have sown. From this day forth your desires, will, and life are yours to command. Embrace yourself and all the magnificence you are—superstar. So mote it be."

"Superstar huh," Mandy giggle, then winked at Lady Maveen. "With the lightening of this candle, I endow myself to embrace and own my innate power. I claim it as my own, banishing all the past defenselessness I have sown. From this day forth my desires, will and life are mine to command. I embrace myself and my superstar magnificence. So mote it be."

Lady Maveen closed her eyes and stood quietly. "I sense there is more that needs to be said. I hear your doubts about finding a good man cawing inside you, just like a crow. This spell will empower you, but if we don't cage the crow, the only man you will be spending time with is your BOB."

"OMG I can't believe you just said that." Mandy's laugh filled the room as she bent over holding her stomach. "BOB has been good to me for many years," she said through her laughter.

Lady Maveen giggled. "Ah child my BOB has been good to me too, but baby girl you need the real thing this time."

Lady Maveen walked out of the room and into the main store. A few minutes later she reappeared holding something in her hand. "This should seal the deal." She held out her hand. "Take this and put it on Mandy."

Mandy grasped a beautiful necklace. The chain a bright silver with a flat ruby gem attached. Inside the ruby a sexy, dancing woman was etched in amethyst. "Wow this is gorgeous." Mandy secured the chain around her neck. "Thank you."

Lady Maveen nodded. "You are welcome. Wear this pendent for the next week and say this spell once a night. It will take root in your heart empowering you to be genuinely free to love and be loved again."

"I will Lady." Mandy turned and faced the altar. "Ready when you are. In fact, I've never been so ready."

Lady Maveen turned towards Mandy. "This time we face each other." She reached out and took Mandy's hands in hers. "Let's begin. As before, repeat the spell."

"Ready."

"You will walk beside your man—together, yet apart. Sharing life, love and each other's hearts. You own yourself, and he owns himself, yet together you are powerfully one. Go forth now and find this man. He is waiting for you. I sense him near, so release your fear. Go with what comes to you. Don't fight it, or forevermore you will rue, this I say as true. So mote it be."

Mandy squeezed Rorry's hands. "I will walk beside my man—together, yet apart. Sharing life, love and each other's hearts. I own myself and he owns himself, yet together we are powerfully one. I go forth now to find this man. He is waiting for me. I sense him near and release my fear. I go with what comes to me, not fighting it, or forevermore, I will rue, this I say as true. So mote it be."

"Well done Mandy."

The two powerful witches hugged each with tears in their eyes. Mandy stepped back. "Now I've got some shopping to do before I go find this mystery man." She winked.

"Oh, that kind of shopping. I think I've got just what you need. Follow me." Lady Maveen led Mandy to beautiful room off the side of the main store area. It was filled with lingerie and everything a sexy witch would need for a night, or life filled with passion.

Mandy felt excitement coarse through her as she tried on an assortment of sexy clothes, bras and panties. Two hours later, she walked out of the Goddess Crone wearing her favorite items and carrying two large shopping bags.

Her mind trickled back to the sexy state trooper who had pulled her over earlier. She glanced at the clock in the Mercedes as she turned the key and started the engine.

"Wow, it's 4:30 already. I guess time flies when you get your sexy back on." She stomped down on the accelerator with her four inch clear plastic stilettos. Just the kind of pumps a sexy stripper would wear. She lowered the top and headed for home.

FOUR

Kit Montaque raced around the kitchen like a crazy woman. It was nearly 5:00PM and the guests for Mandy's 50th surprise party would soon be here.

Kit's boyfriend, Frank Cassidy, was outside firing up the grill and setting out the poolside tables.

The Greyhound Gang made up of Kat, Kelsey, Kirby, Flash, Windy and Hood meandered about the house, waiting for Winter Wonderland to arrive. The dogs got along famously and had been responsible for helping to rescue Connie Griffith when she was kidnapped.

Kit's cell phone rang on the counter. "Hello."

"Hey girlfriend I'm on the way home. I can't wait to tell you what happened today with Lady Maveen. I feel like a new woman!" Mandy giggled softly.

Kit grinned from ear to ear. "Oh my gosh, you sound like a new woman. There's a spark in your voice I haven't heard in at least a year! I can't wait to hear all about it. When do you think you'll be home?" Kit glanced at the clock. It was now five minutes after five in the evening.

"I'm just getting on 287, and barring any delays, I should be home in about an hour." Mandy glanced in her rearview mirror checking for the blue and red lights that would give her the delay she wished for.

"Sounds good, I bought some food for the grill and Frank is firing it up as we speak. Should be ready by the time you get here."

While still on the phone with Mandy, Kit's kitchen door burst open and in walked Connie Griffith, Kandy Hart and Niki Emerson all members of the philanthropic group called The Double Winker's Club. The only member missing was the birthday girl.

Kit held her finger to her lips indicating that they should be quiet. She pointed to the phone and mouthed, 'Mandy.'

The three women tip toed in and quietly greeted all the greyhounds who were doing their doggie greeting dance around the kitchen. Winter raced in, tail wagging and joined the pack of her greyhound friends.

"Sounds perfect, I'll see you soon."

Kit hung up smiling. "Hi girls! That was Mandy, who should be home in about an hour. So we have a little time to get this shindig ready."

"I hope Mandy's okay with this," Connie said as she set a bottle of white wine down on the table.

"She has been dreading this birthday," Kandy said grimly.

"Well, I don't know what happened, but she sounded like a new woman on the phone just now. Something to do with Lady Maveen. Don't know what went on, but whatever it was, it was good."

"Lady who?" said Niki sarcastically.

Connie, Kit and Kandy stopped everything they were doing and turned to stare at Niki.

"I thought you learned your smart mouth lesson at the spa," Kit said.

"I'll be more than happy to refresh your memory if need be," said Connie.

"Seriously Niki, don't start up with your crap tonight." Kandy shook her head. "We love you, but we are kind of done with how you mock anything to do with the craft."

Niki held up her hands, her face was beet red and sweating. "No, I didn't mean it to come out that way. Really!" She gathered her friends in a group hug. "I did learn my lesson and you mean the world to me. You are my family."

Kit visibly relaxed as she hugged the youngest of the group back. "Maybe we've gotten hypersensitive, and for that I apologize."

"Me too," Connie said.

"Me three," Kandy echoed.

Connie broke open the bottle of wine as Kit pulled four glasses from the cabinet.

"To us!" Niki said.

The girls clinked their wine glasses together and took a sip.

"To The Double Winker's Club!" Kit held her glass in the air.

Frank walked into the kitchen just as the smiling women lowered their glasses.

"Drinking so early ladies?" He smiled, lighting up his handsome face.

Kit picked up a glass she'd poured for her man and handed it to him. "You know us honey, any excuse for a party."

"Speaking of the party girl, when is she due in? I want to make sure I don't start the food too soon." Frank took a long sip of the wine.

"She just called and said her ETA is one hour." Kit rubbed Franks back. "Thanks for doing the food honey."

Frank winked. "Anything for you baby."

The other ladies rolled their eyes while simultaneously smiling at the sappy duo.

"So what can I help you with?" Kandy asked.

"Can you put the veggies and dip on the platter?" Kit opened the fridge and pulled out the fresh vegetables, handing them to Kandy.

Together, like a fine tuned machine, the members of The Double Winker's Club went to work. Mandy's party was set to be a fun night, filled with the love of her best friends.

FIVE

All he could think about was her. She was beyond beautiful, and like an idiot he'd let her get away. He sat glumly in his cruiser halfheartedly running radar.

She was a piece of him that had been missing for so long. He glanced down at her information that he'd written down on a small note pad. At least he had her name and address. He could definitely find...the radar suddenly went off, screaming like a banshee.

He looked first to the radar reading of 90 mph and then out the windshield. He smiled as a blur of white flashed by him. Could he really be this lucky?

Flipping on the overhead emergency lights and siren, he eased the cruiser out of the hiding place and onto the highway.

It didn't take him long to get right behind the suspect vehicle, a 2012 Mercedes. He watched as the driver glanced in her rearview mirror. He could swear he saw her smiling.

Her long hair flew wildly in the wind as the Mercedes eased over two lanes and onto to the shoulder, coming to a stop quickly.

He put his cruiser in park and got out slowly. She watched him in the mirror as he walked to the driver's side of her car. He looked down at the stunning woman, noticing the new sexy white button down shirt that barely reached the top of her short jean skirt. She looked good enough to eat, literally. His cock filled his tight blue uniform pants.

"Ms. Devine, we meet again." He glanced down at the beautiful woman he'd just been fantasizing about moments before. "You were going 90. Is there someplace you need to be?" Gosh he hoped not.

She looked up at him, and then slowly took off her mirrored aviator sunglasses. Amazing clear blue eyes focused on him.

"I am sorry! I had no idea how fast I was going. You hardly feel the speed in this car." She pulled out her license and cards and started to hand them to him.

He held up his hand. "That won't be necessary. I already have your information. I'm going to have to issue you a warning. Wait here please."

Her shoulders sagged and she slipped her sunglasses back on covering those gorgeous eyes. "So much for Lady Maveen's mojo," she mumbled."

A few minutes later, he walked back to the sports car and handed her the warning ticket. "This doesn't go on your record and you won't get any points. Please drive slower in the future Ms. Devine." With his hand he signaled her to wait and walked back to his cruiser. He got in and shut off the overhead emergency lights. He didn't want his next move on the dash cam for all the haters he had in the department to see. Through the windshield, he saw her watching his every move. Summoning up his courage he got out and walked back to her car.

He crouched down, balancing on his feet as he came face to face with his dream girl. "So Ms. Devine you never answered my question."

Mandy folded the warning and put it on the passenger seat. "What question is that Trooper Reyes-Mythos?"

He smiled brightly, "My name is Therron, but you can call me Jessie."

Eyebrows raised she looked back at the intriguing man. "Therron, but you can call me Jessie? Really?"

"It's a long story; let's just say Jessie is a much easier name to remember." He thought back to the 80's when a certain song had made all the ladies swoon. Nobody could ever pronounce Therron correctly, much less remember it, so he'd changed it. Not like it mattered. He'd just started another new life, with new "friends," and a new job. His consciousness came back to the present as he heard her talking.

"Jessie's a nice name. I always loved that song," she said. "Now what was that question again?"

"Are you heading anywhere special?" His eyes locked onto hers, his gaze going right through their sunglasses.

Her chest heaved with a deep breath. Quickly, she composed herself again.

"Actually I think my friends are giving me a little surprise party tonight. I just got off the phone with my best friend Kit, and it sounded pretty busy in the background."

He took off his sunglasses and anchored them on his shirt. Desire glazed over his eyes, and he ran his tongue over his teeth. Did he dare? Normally shy, his inner hunter was pushing him to go for it. "Come out with me tonight. I promise you a night you will never forget."

Mandy swallowed deeply. "I would hate to disappoint my friends." Her breathing was quick and shallow. "Then again, they've been telling me I needed to have some fun."

He leaned in closer. "I promise you fun beyond your wildest dreams." He glanced at his watch. "It's 5:45, I'm off in fifteen minutes. How about you following me to the barracks so I can get out of this monkey suit and then we can leave from there? I'm sure your friends will understand."

She nodded, as though in a trance and whispered. "Okay."

He got back in his car then waved his hand out the window for her to follow as he eased out into traffic.

SIX

Mandy's legs shook with nervous excitement as she pushed down on the gas pedal and followed the cruiser. Traffic actually came to a stop to let the two cars back onto the busy highway.

Holy smokes, was she really going to do this with a complete stranger? Really, what was she doing? Probably dinner and—no way, the guy was smoking hot and looked to be in his early 30's. What would he want with her?

"Call Kit," she said out loud. The car's speaker rang three times while she waited in guilty anticipation. It caught her off guard when a deep male voice answered.

"Yo, birthday girl, where you at?" said the distinct voice of Kit's boyfriend, Trooper Frank Cassidy.

"U'm, hi Frank, is Kit there?"

"You sound funny Mandy, is everything alright?" His voice switched from Kit's boyfriend to state trooper mode.

"No, nothing like that Frank. I'm fine, really. Can I talk to Kit for a minute?" Her faced grew hot as she thought about what she was going to tell her. She tapped her sport length bright pink nails on the wheel.

"Oh I see girl talk. Just tell me one thing."

"What Frank?"

"Do I start grilling the food or not?"

She heard a slap and Frank grunted.

Here's Kit, and, whatever you're up to, have fun, Birthday Girl."

Mandy heard Kit mumble something to Frank and then come on the phone. "Hi, Mandy. What's going on?"

"Remember when you all told me I needed to get my sexy back with a hot young stud?" Mandy said

"I remember saying something to that effect at the party last year," Kit said.

"Well, I..."

Kit stopped her midsentence. "Hold on a minute this has to be on speaker phone."

Mandy just about died as she heard the phone clunk down on a hard surface and Kit reminding the girls about the end of the party toast last year.

"Okay go ahead girlfriend," Kit said.

"I am not going to say another word until you tell me Frank is out of the room and that only members of the Double Winker's Club are there."

"Yes to both," Connie said happily.

"Come on Mandy we're dying to know what is going on!" Kandy said eagerly.

"This is gonna be good," Niki said.

"Spill the beans, Sista," Kit said enthusiastically.

"Okay, okay," Mandy said giggling. "I got pulled over by a gorgeous state trooper this morning. Remember Kit?"

"Oh I remember. Did he give you a little parting gift?"

"Not the first time, but the second time he pulled me over."

"Twice!" her friends said in unison.

"I was going 90 at the time. So yeah, twice." Mandy continued telling her friends' as she signaled and took the exit off the highway right behind the troop car. "Ladies when I say this man is beyond gorgeous, I am not lying!"

"And..." said Connie.

"And after he gave me a written warning, he asked me to go out with him tonight. He's promised me a night of my dreams. I'm following him to the barracks now. Would you guys be really mad at me if I didn't come home for a few hours? I know you planned something for me and..."

"Heck no!" said Kandy.

"Enjoy your stud!" said Kit.

"Make sure he rubbers up for safety!" Connie said.

"Oh my gosh, it's just dinner!" Mandy inhaled sharply. "Why would a thirty year old stud want to have sex with me on the eve of my half a century old birthday?" Half of her believed that, and half of her was praying she was dead wrong.

"I am not going to dignify that with a response. Like Connie said, you make sure to practice safe sex with your stud!"

"We will reschedule this shindig for tomorrow. That is if you can walk," Niki said.

"You girls are crazy and I love you! Thanks for understanding. I am going to hang up now because we are pulling into the barracks."

"Have fun with the stud!" Connie said. "Hey, just in case he turns out to be a serial killer what's his name?"

Mandy snorted. "Yeah a hunky serial killer stalks his victims in a state trooper car. His names Therron Reyes-Mythos, but he calls himself Jessie."

"Wow that's a mouth full. I hope he lives up to his name if you know what I mean," Kandy said.

"Yeah if he's too small throw him back. You know like a fish." Niki shrugged.

"Jessie is a sexy name. Me likey," Connie said.

"I hope he can survive her! She hasn't been out for a ride in a long time," Kandy said.

"I pity the poor fool," Kit said through her giggles.

"Yee haw!" Niki yelled.

Connie yelled good bye into the phone as Mandy hung up gliding the Roadster into an empty space.

He was at her door in a matter of seconds. "I'll only be a few minutes. Would you rather wait here or inside?"

"Um, I think I'll wait here."

"I won't be long. Don't you dare leave!"

"No way. How can I resist your promise of a wild night of my dreams?"

He blushed a bright red as he backed away, then turned and entered the station.

SEVEN

He walked into the barracks with a spring in his step and a smile on his face. That is until he turned the corner and saw his worst nightmares standing there.

Trooper Larry Powers turned from looking out the window. "Who's the broad in the banging Mercedes vampire boy?"

Jessie brushed past him without bothering to answer. Powers had made this life a living hell for him ever since he'd witnessed him healing a vampire, who was bleeding out at an accident. Not that he realized what he'd actually seen, but ever since that night Jessie had been labeled a freak.

"What's the matter Mythos black cat got your tongue?"

"Fuck you, Powers!"

The other troopers laughed as he gave them the finger and walked into the locker room.

What he wouldn't give to be able to start this lifetime over. He'd have been so much more careful. Powers never would have seen a thing and his label of freak wouldn't exist. Unfortunately not even vampires got do over's.

He showered and changed into stone washed jeans, a tight black tee shirt, and brown cowboy boots. He glanced at himself in the mirror and frowned. One thing was for sure he had enough good looks to go around and no one to share them with.

He smiled remembering just who was waiting for him in the parking lot. Exiting the locker room he walked back out and into an empty room. Where the hell were his hecklers?

Through the barracks rear window he spied them gathered around the white Roadster. Inside the convertible his girl didn't look happy.

He raced outside. She was talking, but he couldn't hear what she was saying. He reached the car just as she uttered, "So mote it be."

The four troopers gathered around her suddenly turned and waved, smiling at him as he approached.

"Hey Jessie, this gal is a keeper!"

"You lucky dog, have a great night," said Larry Powers.

The other two patted him on the back as they passed him on their way back into the station.

What the hell? He wondered and looked at Mandy, shrugged his shoulders, and gave her a 'what was that about' look.

She smiled and winked. "For me to know and you to enjoy for the next week." She laughed happily. "So where to, my handsome young stud?

He smiled back at the beautiful woman—his woman—only she didn't quite know it as yet. "First, I am going to feed you because you are going to need some strength for later." Desire flashed across his handsome face as he opened her car door. "Let's take my car and then we can come back for yours after dinner."

Mandy eyed his toned body up and down, his desire mirrored in her face. "I'm all yours for the next few hours." She got out and stood up next to him, her eyes level with his juicy red lips.

"Oh Mandy, we are going to need much more than just a few hours." Taking her hand he guided her over to a brand new black Camaro with dark tinted windows all around. It was built just like its owner, lean, sleek and screaming sex.

He opened the passenger door and waited for Mandy to get in, and then closed it. It shut with a solid thud sealing her in. There was no turning back now. Tonight was going to be magical, wild and freeing for the both of them. This he vowed as he opened the door and got behind the wheel of the new muscle car.

EIGHT

They watched him from the shadows as he put the girl in his car and went around to the driver's side. He stopped for a moment, smelling the air as if sensing their presence.

They stiffened against the tree until he got behind the wheel and started the car. He had plans for tonight, well so did they. He'd been getting closer and closer to their lair and it was going to stop tonight. Therron Reyes-Mythos was a powerful hunter and healer of the Queens elite guard. He was someone, the less than honest vampires feared and admired at the same time.

The profession had been passed down from his father, a very powerful vampire in the Adulane race. Therron, however, was even more powerful than his father Zacharis, for he possessed the blood of his mother, a powerful witch called Raven Reyes. She had been the High Priestess of the Santigo Coven, but had gone missing shortly after his birth.

Their orders were clear he was not to survive the night. Healer or not, tonight he was the hunted.

With swoosh of their long cloaks the three vampires disappeared into the darkening night.

NINE

Mandy sat beside the handsome stranger barely able to conceal her anticipation. The girls had been right. She needed the company of a younger, sexy as hell, man. Whatever tonight was to bring, she was going to enjoy every second of it for come the morning light, she would never see him again.

He looked over and smiled. Picking up her hand he brought it to his mouth and gently kissed her palm.

Tingles shot out from her; long dormant sexual desire filling her body with a feeling of lust that she never thought she'd feel again. She didn't care that he was young enough to be her son, she was going to let loose and be a wild woman. If the mere touch of his lips to her palm was an indication of his prowess, she was going to have the time of her life.

Taking his thumb she guided it to her mouth and sucked it inside. Tickling the tip with her tongue she moved his thumb in and out of her warm mouth, lost in her imagination of another part of his body in its place.

Suddenly they were stopped on the side of the road and he was kissing her, shoving his moist tongue into her mouth, simulating what he would be doing to her sex later.

"Shoot, I'm not sure I'm going to make it through dinner." She kissed him back playfully, running her tongue over his teeth. Surprise shot through her as she felt two pointed teeth on each side of his mouth.

He hesitated when she stopped kissing him back and slowly opened his eyes. Looking through hooded lids at her he softly said, "Scared Mandy?

Her body felt like quivering jelly as she nodded, then grabbed his hair pulled him forward. She crushed her mouth to his, licking and kissing playfully, she teased him with her tongue while watching his eyes glaze over. Releasing him, she leaned back. "Scared, Jessie?"

A grin covered his chiseled face as he shifted gears and edged the Camaro off the shoulder and onto the road again. "Oh, you have no idea baby. What would you like to eat, besides me?"

"Athletes stock up on carbs before a big workout so I'm thinking pasta would be a yummy idea." She exhaled softly. "Just kissing you is enough to zap my strength."

"Well, we wouldn't want that. There is so much more we're going to do tonight. Pasta it is."

Mandy looked over the dash of the sports car. There was a two way hard wired radio and the car appeared to be set up as a patrol cruiser. "Wow, you have a lot of interesting gadgets in this car. Do you have to respond when you are off duty?"

Therron smiled. "Actually I have a side security business. I have to be ready to go at a moment's notice if a client calls." He squeezed her hand gently. "Ready to go get some food?" he asked, dropping the subject.

Mandy nodded as he eased the car back onto the roadway. The powerful engine filling the air with a sexy, thready sound.

They rode in pleasant silence for several miles until the Camaro turned into a quaint Italian eatery's parking lot.

The restaurant's atmosphere was dark and seductive, with only candle light glowing from the tables and a fire place to provide light. They were seated in a quiet booth near the crackling fire.

He treated her like a real date. Waiting for her to be seated first, letting her order before him and having eyes only for her. Too bad she'd never see him again, she thought.

Looking over the table at the beautiful blonde before him his thoughts went wild. He had no idea of what her tastes were in regard to sex in this lifetime. Was she wild and free, or just the missionary position type girl? Either way he'd take her.

"Perhaps we should set some ground rules for tonight," he said kissing her hand.

"Ground rules?" Mandy leaned forward.

"Mandy I'm a very sensual person and I enjoy a variety of pleasures when it comes to sexual pairing."

"Sexual pairing. Now that's romantic," she said sarcastically.

Shit his age was showing. "What I meant was that I want to please you tonight. I don't want to do anything that you don't want me to. That's what I meant by ground rules."

She felt wild and ready for anything as she got up and sat down next to him in the booth. Without a care to anyone else she kissed him deeply. "I want you for my birthday present tonight." She nipped his lip.

"I'd love to be your birthday present, Mandy." He leaned back in the booth and caught his breath. His cock strained against his jeans. "I know you say that now, but just in case let's have a safe word you can say if you want me to stop."

Her eyes grew wide as the ramification of his words hit her. What the hell was she doing? Mandy Devine didn't have sex with random men, especially one she needed a safe word with. "U'm, maybe this isn't such a great idea and. I should go home after dinner."

Pain covered his face. "Go home? We just found each other. Please don't be scared. I won't do anything that you don't want. You are an amazing woman and I will treat you as nothing less than a Goddess."

Her goodie two shoes and devilish sides fought a good battle, with the devilish side winning. "I don't know why, but I trust you. After all we only have this one night so why not? Since you have experience in this kind of "sexual pairing", what's a good, safe word?"

He snorted softly. "I'm never going to live that one down." Holding her hand he caressed her palm. "How about pasta," he said.

"Pasta? That's not very romantic."

"Mandy, safe words are words you'd never use during sex. I mean, unless of course there is something you need to tell me?" He laughed and his smile met his eyes.

Mandy gulped. "So, a safe word is what I say if I want you to stop doing something?"

Jessie nodded. "Now you've got it. My tastes run the full gamut and I want you to feel safe that nothing will happen that you don't want." He locked eyes with hers.

Mandy's eyes widened as she locked onto his gaze. This was no ordinary man. "U'm, your eyes are kind of glowing. They look like hot amber."

"My eyes have been known to turn a color or two depending on my mood. Right now, my eyes are matching how friggin' hot and turned on I am. You are the sexiest woman I've seen in a long, long time."

The waitress cleared her throat as she approached their table. "Anything else?" She smiled and blushed at the sheer sexual desire on the man's face. It was gone the minute he looked up at her.

"No, thank you. Just the check please." He looked back at Mandy. "Ready?"

Mandy inhaled deeply to steady herself and shook her head indicating she was ready to leave. Words stuck in her throat as she realized dinner was over and it was literally time for dessert.

He paid the check and stood up waiting for Mandy .

"I'm shaking, Jessie," she said as she stood up.

Taking her arm in his, he winked. "Baby, you are going to be shaking all over when I'm done with you."

"Pasta?"

He shook his head. "Only if you're still hungry for food?"

She shook with anticipation as they slowly walked out arm and arm and got into the Camaro.

TEN

"Well I guess the party is off." Kit shook her head. "All this planning and poof!"

Connie nodded. "You have to admit it is for a good cause."

Kandy snorted and soda shot out of her nose. She coughed and sputtered as Niki patted her on the back.

Frank walked into the room just as the girls burst out laughing. He turned around and walked back outside, flipping open his phone. He needed some testosterone to arrive and soon!

Kit crept up behind him as he was putting his phone to his ear. She wrapped her arms around him and smiled as the big state trooper jumped.

"Holy heck, woman you scared me!" He slammed his phone shut. "I was just calling to see when some male reinforcements are going to get here. I'm out numbered!" He kissed her softly on her mouth. "Then again maybe you and I should go upstairs."

Kit ran her fingers up and down her mans toned chest. "Last one to the bed has to do everything I tell him too." She took off in a dead run yelling out orders to her friends.

Frank ran in after her, and right into the girls of The Double Winker's Club.

"Where ya going in such a hurry, Frank?" Connie said as she grabbed his arm.

"Why don't you sit down and chat with us for a while. You can fill me in on all the latest state trooper stuff." Officer Kandy Hart, of the Wayne PD, smiled up at the handsome man.

Niki pulled out a chair. "Why don't you have a seat?"

Frank grinned, and did moves worthy of an all-star football player. He was out of their grasps and racing up the stairs. "Montaque you play dirty! Not as dirty as me though."

The girls smiled as they heard the bedroom door slam.

"I have to admit, I am very jealous of Kit and Mandy tonight," Kandy said.

Connie and Niki nodded.

"Since this shindig is off, how about we break out some old games to play." Connie walked into the family room and opened a cabinet.

Niki and Kandy followed.

"I vote for UNO," said Niki.

"UNO it is." Connie grabbed the UNO game and pulled it out. Looking at her two friends, she shook her head. "Can you believe that the three of us are sitting around playing games instead of having hot steamy sex with a gorgeous guy?"

Niki sighed and plopped down on a chair at the game table. "What a bunch of losers we are."

Kandy poured herself a rum and coke. "What can I get you other losers?"

The three women burst out laughing.

"I'm going to have Mandy whip up some kind of love potion for me." Kandy sipped her drink.

"Oh, come on, don't tell me you two believe in all that witchcraft stuff!" Niki shook her head.

"After what happened when Mandy, Kandy and Kit saved me from the kidnappers, I'm a believer!" Connie sat down in the chair opposite Niki. "I don't blame you Niki, because you weren't around for the whole thing, but I tell you, there was magic in the air that night, and it saved my ass."

Kandy patted Connie's shoulder. "I was a newbie then and wasn't sure what I believed, but now look at me." She pointed to the silver amulet around her neck. "I'm a full member of Mandy's Coven and learning more and more each day. It is real, Sister."

Niki rolled her eyes. "Believe what you will. I don't fault either of you. It's just that I don't believe in anything supernatural. As far as I am concerned, God created we humans and the assorted animal species on this earth, and that's it. Witchcraft is all in your minds and so is any other demonic craft."

Kandy and Connie turned to the younger woman with eyes glaring.

"Are you saying you think how I believe and live now is demonic?" Kandy snarled.

"How dare you say something like that to us, Niki? We have a right to our beliefs and way of life just like you do. For you to insinuate that this has something to do with demons is beyond pissing me off." Connie stood up. "I think I'll be going now."

Niki stood up and tried to stop Connie. "Wait I didn't mean it like that."

Connie brushed by her, as did Kandy. The two of them grabbed their coats, purses and keys and walked out the door.

Niki stood there looking forlorn just as Kit and Frank walked back into the kitchen.

"Where did everybody go?" Frank raised his hands in question.

"Um...." Niki stammered.

"Let me guess, your mouth got you in trouble again and cleared the room. Unbelievable, Niki! When are you going to grow up and start caring about what comes out of your mouth?" Kit shook her head fiercely.

"Baby, I'm going to grill up some veggies and some of those vegetarian chick fillets. I'll be grilling just enough for two." He glared at Niki.

"Fine, I get the hint. Just because I said I thought witchcraft is demonic, you all go bonkers on me. Have it your way, I'm out of here." Niki grabbed her things and stomped out of the house.

"Great party." Kit threw the hors d'oeuvres in a bowl and then into the fridge. "Great to find out that one of my friends thinks I'm a demon, too. Wow! I can't believe that girl!"

Frank wrapped his arms around his lady. "The only place I think you are a demon, is in bed and I like that." He kissed her softly on the forehead. "Don't worry, you girls will work this out, you always do." He carried the plate of veggies and chick fillets outside to the grill.

Kit leaned back against the counter. "I'm not so sure. This time Niki may have gone too far," she whispered.

ELEVEN

Jesse turned the souped up Camaro into the parking lot of a store called Black Velvet and parked in a space by the door. Looking over at Mandy he gave her a sexy grin. "I have a few things to pick up for tonight beautiful."

Desire crawled up her legs and into her soft mound of sex. "I've never been in a store like this before."

He leaned over the console and kissed her. "You wait here. Since I am your birthday present let me do the shopping." He winked and got out of the car.

She inhaled deeply his sexy aftershave clouding her senses. She was really doing this! Turning on the radio she leaned back in the seat and closed her eyes. Imagination took over as she thought about everything she wanted to do to Jessie tonight. Fearless. Fearless. Fearless.

She didn't know how long she'd been day dreaming when the driver's door opened and Jessie got in the car. He leaned back and carefully put a bag onto the rear seat. Putting the key in the ignition, he started the engine and then took Mandy's hand into his. "I'll take you to get your car and you can follow me to the place I have all picked out."

"Sounds like a plan," she said with more bravado than she felt.

Several minutes later they pulled into the trooper barracks and he stopped next to her car. He opened the door and got out, coming around to her side. Opening her door, he stretched out his hand. Grasping it, she let him help her out of the low riding vehicle.

Mandy pushed the automatic start on the key chain and the Mercedes engine came to life. She opened her door and slid behind the wheel.

"How does the GPS work in this car?" When Therron leaned inside the car his body brushed against Mandy, who speechlessly, pointed to a place on the dash. He studied it for a minute and then keyed in a destination address. "I want you to follow what the GPS says and I will be behind you. Remember I'm an officer of the law and you are to obey everything and anything I tell you to."

Without another word, he stood up and closed her door. Going to his vehicle he got in and waited for her to do as he had instructed.

Mandy froze behind the wheel, momentarily caught off guard. Just what did the sexy stud have planned for her tonight? Her logical mind fought back and forth for a few seconds until she remembered her power word again—Fearless. Backing slowly out she locked eyes with Jessie, sitting behind the wheel of his Camaro and smiled.

The GPS put her back on the highway for several miles until it told her to take the next exit. Signaling, she eased off the accelerator and let the sports car handle the curve in the exit ramp. Coming to a stop at the bottom of the ramp, she found herself in a very desolate and wooded area.

She turned right, continuing to follow the GPS instructions as it took her down a series of roads until she came to a large gated driveway. Raven's Hood Manor was written on a hand painted sign, hanging from a tree. Stopping the Mercedes she watched as the heavy, dark, metallic gate slid open by its own volition.

The gravel crinkled underneath the tires of the SL 550 as she drove down the long dark driveway. It felt like miles before she finally saw an old stone manor with a barn next to it. The barn door stood open and there was a dim light glowing from inside it. She was about to stop and get out when a spotlight came on from the Camaro behind her.

"Drive your car into the barn." Jessie's sexy voice said over the Camaro's PA system. "Pull all the way into the back of the barn and then shut off your vehicle and get out."

Mandy swallowed hard wondering once again if she was crazy for going through with this. Once she drove all the way into the barn, she realized that there was no going back. She gathered her courage, took a deep breath and drove all the way through the barn to the rear of the long building, chanting to herself, "Fearless...Fearless...Fearless."

Stopping, she shut off the engine and cautiously got out of the Mercedes. Glancing around through the dim light, she noticed small lanterns hanging from the rafters, all evenly spaced, ten in all. The lighting created an atmosphere that was a perfect setting for a seduction. She stood beside the white car, her excitement mingling with the fear coursing through her body as she waited and wondered what was going to happen next.

The souped up Camaro idled at the doorway, then slowly drove through, Jesse stopped a car length away from the SL 550. The sports car's engine shut down. She couldn't see Jessie through the black tinted windows, but strangely, she could feel his energy; vital, sensual, demanding.

Mandy felt her nipples hardened beneath her new red lace bra. This was the first time in a very long while she felt her sex center dampened with desire. What is he waiting for?

The Camaro's PA system crackled to life. "Miss, go stand at the rear of your vehicle and wait for further instructions."

Since she hadn't worn four inch, fuck me, pumps in a very long time, she found herself having to walk gingerly so she didn't break her neck while walking in the dim light. Once she reached the back she faced Jessie's car. This felt all too real like she was being pulled over by a handsome trooper and about to find out what he wanted.

The Camaro's driver's door opened and Jessie eased out. He left the door open as he fingered what appeared to be a gun holstered to his belt.

"Holy shit Jessie!" He was all business, and Mandy began to get frightened and back away. She kept moving until stopping dead, as the bumper of her car pushed into her bare legs.

"Miss, please stop trying to get away. I don't want to hurt you." He winked as if to let her know this was all an act and part of her birthday dessert. "Please move forward and stand there. "He pointed to a place approximately five feet in front of him.

Mandy walked forward to the point and stopped. "Why did you pull me over trooper? Was I doing something wrong?" she asked, deciding to get into the act.

Jessie leaned back against the hood of his vehicle and smiled. "No, but you are going to have to do something for me if you want to go free tonight."

His eyes practically undressed her as he looked up and down her body. A faint drop of sweat glistened between her breasts as she looked down.

"What is your name?"

"Mandy Devine, sir."

"Well Mandy, I'm in need of some release tonight and it looks like you are going to provide that for me. Do we have an understanding?"

She nodded.

"Good." He walked back to his car and leaned in and turned on the dashboard camcorder. "I'll make sure you get a copy so you can always remember our time together."

Mandy's sex started to tingle as the ramifications of what they were doing became clear. "I'll do anything you want trooper, to get out of the ticket. I can't afford another one."

His hard on jumped in his pants fighting to get free of the restraining fabric. "Just the words I like to hear, Mandy. Do you promise to do everything I tell you to?"

She nodded.

"I'm sorry, I didn't hear you?"

"Yes, I promise," she said.

He walked over to her and leaned down next to her ear. "Very good," he whispered softly. He stood behind her and edged his leg between hers. "I'm going to pat you down for any weapons."

Her fun button nearly exploded as his hands came around the front of her and ran down her throat, under her shirt, bra and onto the raw flesh of her breasts.

He kneaded them softly, pulling back with a deep exhalation. Continuing their exploration, his hands proceeded slowly down to her stomach. They stopped when they reached the end of her jean skirt. "One last chance. Say stop now or there is no going back beautiful."

Her breathing fast and shallow escalated as she whispered, "I want you, Jessie."

He kissed the back of her neck then moved to her right ear. His warm breath floated across her ear lobe and down the passage. "You won't be sorry."

Grabbing the end of her skirt in both hands he pulled it up. His rock hard shaft twitched as he pulled her gently into him. He inhaled sharply as his fingers felt a G-string covering her moist triangle. Slowly he pushed beneath the narrow band and ran his fingers down the short trimmed landing strip of hair. Barely able to stop, he pulled his hand out and stepped away from Mandy.

She nearly fell as her legs seemed to have turned to jelly from his touch. He reached out to steady her. "Now Ms. Devine I want you to stand in front of the car and do everything I tell you to, exactly the way I tell you to. Do you understand?"

"Yes," she said breathlessly.

He moved backwards and leaned against the hood of his car, staring at her. "Unbutton your top very slowly." His eyes were locked on her breasts as her fingers slowly undid the first button, then the second button, the third button, fourth, then the fifth button, and finally the last one.

His eyes glazed over seductively as he saw the blood red lace bra she was wearing. Her breasts practically spilled out of it and the tip of her dark areola crested the top. Holy hell, he hadn't realized that his woman had such a beautiful rack and he hadn't even seen the whole package yet.

"Take your shirt off and drop it to the floor." His eyes never left her as she slowly slid the shirt down her arms and let it drop onto the floor. She then stood before him with a lacy wisp of red barely concealing her beautiful breasts. "Very nice," he commented, "and just the right size."

His gaze lowered to her skirt. "Slip that skirt down and step out of it so I can see all of you." He watched as she wiggled seductively while she slowly pushed the skirt down. It finally dropped to the floor and she stepped out of it.

Concealed only by a sliver of red lace fabric, her love triangle dripped moist beads down her legs. "I can't wait to see just what is underneath the lace." He motioned with his hands to circle around.

She swiveled around facing the trunk of her Mercedes. He made her wait several seconds before he continued.

"Move forward and bend over the top of your trunk. Very good. Now spread your legs." He pushed away from the hood of his car and came up behind her and pressed his fully clothed body against her nearly naked one. "You are so friggin' beautiful."

His hands came around her and she nearly jumped when he seized each breast. She felt her desire escalated even further when he took her nipples between his fingers and pinched them hard.

Her fun button contracted and an orgasm wracked through her body. She could barely stand up as he moved even closer to steady her. "Jessie," she whispered.

Her body came alive, and Mandy truly felt she was young again. This man awakened everything that had been too long dormant inside of her. What a birthday present. Clouded with passion she felt her bra release and be guided down her arms. Her bare tits touched the coolness of the car.

In the distance thunder crackled through the warm August night and rain started drizzling and then become louder as it began to steadily fall outside the open barn door. The fullness of his shaft pressed against her butt as he pushed her - G-string aside and slowly eased his fingers inside her.

"I bought some special warming lube just for you, baby." His fingers glided in and out of her and the warmth spread across her entire sex triangle.

She pushed against his hard-on as he kissed the back of her neck. "I want you Jessie," she whispered passionately.

"Not until you are good and ready, Miss Devine." He pulled his finger out and wrapped his hands around her hips. Kneeling down he twirled her around until her box was against his mouth.

He began licking and nipping and teased her love button until her body shook with another orgasm. Her juices shot out and he licked them up while his tongue continued to work magic on her.

She glanced down at him as he sucked her juices up like a greedy animal. "I want you inside me now!"

"Yes, Mistress." Roughly, he lifted her onto the trunk of the car and spread her legs. She stretched out seductively watching him as he devoured her with his eyes that appeared to glistening in the low light. Behind him, she saw the doorway suddenly ablaze with lightening. Slowly he pulled off his tight black shirt revealing a hairless chest bulging with muscles. He threw the shirt onto the hood of his car and grabbed his zipper. It moved down slowly revealing a huge bulge straining to break free.

Jessie saw that Mandy was almost panting by this time. He smiled and began to slowly push his pants down over his narrow hips, tantalizing her by dropping them only inches at a time. When finally they revealed the magnificent package waiting for her inside black boxer briefs, he heard her suck in her breath. "Still want me inside you Mandy?" His eyes racked her body seductively as he grasp the band holding the briefs up and gave one final push and they were down.

In her wildest male stripper dreams, she'd never imagined a man so finely built. His hard cock twitched as it sprung free. Little drops of cum glistened on its tip as he took it in his hand and slipped a condom on.

"In all my years, I've never wanted a birthday present as much as I've wanted you." She edged her body forward at the same time he did. His cock slowly impaled her until her moistly readied sex allowed full entrance.

They locked eyes as he leaned forward kissing her deeply as he began to thrust. Her ass practically hung in the air as he held her up and slammed into her over and over again.

She grabbed his hair and pulled hard.

His eyes glowed amber once again as he lowered his lips to her neck and nibbled. It took every ounce of his will power not to stick his fangs into her jugular and make her his forever. No, that would be her choice if it ever came down to it, not his!

Rain battered against the barn windows and roof, the pounding crescendo matching theirs. Thundered roared overhead as his climax built.

He moved back up to her lips. She lowered her palm and cupped his balls, squeezing them, as he let out a moan and came hard. His load shot out of him, again and again, filling the condom to capacity. Although his vampire side was immune to disease and could fight anything his human side acquired, he didn't want Mandy to feel concern. Quickly he pulled out and held onto the condom.

Kissing her, he pulled the condom off, then tossed it aside. It landed with a splat on the rear bumper of the Mercedes. He smiled and winked. "A lot of something to remember me by until the next wash."

Mandy closed her legs and slid off the car trunk, landing next to him. He pulled her into his arms and kissed the top of her head. Somehow it felt tender, implying more than the one night stand she knew it really was.

"That was amazing, Birthday Present," she said, gazing up into his eyes.

"That was only part one, of your birthday present." He pulled a pink robe out of one of the Black Velvet bags and wrapped it around her body. "Let's go inside. I have someone I want you to meet."

Mandy stopped short. "U'm, we have just had some mind blowing sex out here in your barn—and I'm only wearing a bathrobe—I really don't think this is the best time for me to meet anyone. What I would really enjoy is a nice hot bath." She shivered against the cool wind the storm had brought along with the rain.

"Oh, she won't mind," he said, guiding her out the door, through the rain and into the kitchen of Raven's Hood Manor.

TWELVE

The two vampires watched the lovers walk out of the barn and enter the manor. It had been quite the show and they both snickered. They intended to make certain Therron would not see another morning, but at least he would go out with a smile on his face.

Together the tall thin men silently skirted the house and entered the barn.

The one named Simon knelt down next to the Camaro. Pulling a small box from his coat he lay down and wiggled underneath the frame. The magnet in the box latched onto the metal undercarriage and secured itself neatly. Pushing a button on the side the box blinked to life and the countdown began.

Edging his way out, he grabbed his partner Kastor's hand, to help him stand up.

Both men knew this mission was of the utmost importance since it would decide their ranking among their gang of Outcast vampires. They were Outcasts from the Adulane Vampire Society for heinous acts against their own kind, humans and an assortment of many other species.

Their survival depended on their skill at tracking down and killing the Adulane's hunters like Therron Reyes-Mythos.

This one might prove a bit trickier than the others because of the witch blood running through his veins. Still, they had all the confidence in the world that they would have their fifth confirmed kill by the morning light.

Bringing back the witch, Mandy Devine would be icing on the cake and insure their rise in the ranks. The things the others would do to her ripe body would make the show they'd just witnessed look like child's play.

The bomb exploding would bring them running to the barn to see what the commotion was and once out in the open they would be easy prey for the Outcasts to take.

The timer was set to go off in exactly thirty minutes which would leave plenty of time for both of them to get in place, ready for action.

Raising their hands, they high fived each other then went off to their separate hiding places to wait for the fun to begin.

The hunter and his new slut won't know what hit them in exactly twenty-nine minutes and four seconds.

THIRTEEN

The coal black raven watched from the rafters of the barn as the two Outcast vampires set up their trap. Silently, she hopped back and forth on the beam, wanting to catch every word of their scheme.

When the men finally exited the barn, she took flight out of the hay barn door and flew up to the open second floor window of her bedroom.

Entering the room, she swooped through the doorway and down the stairs, nearly flying beak first into Therron and his pretty little witch.

Landing squarely on Therron's shoulder, she cawed once as a startled Mandy jumped backwards.

Therron smiled at her, and then turned to his witch. "Mandy, I'd like you to meet Lady Raven, principal witch of the Santigo coven, and also my mom.

Mandy backed away until her butt hit the foyer wall. Holy shit, she'd just fucked a certified psycho who thought a bird was his mother. "Ah, yeah right. I think I best be going Jessie, Therron or whatever your name is."

Panic was apparent on his face as he realized what an idiot he was to be introducing the raven as his Mother, even if she really was. "Wait Mandy, let me explain."

"Enough! There is no time for you to bicker or have a mental break down. I have come to tell you that there are two Outcasts waiting outside for you right now. There is a bomb planted underneath your car, and when it goes off they are going to kill you, my son, and take your witch and use her for their pleasure." The raven flew off his shoulder and onto the window sill.

Mandy's eyes grew wide and she froze where she stood as her brain attempted to rationalize the fact that a big, black crow was talking. "Okay wake up," Mandy said, "Wake up! This must all be some really great dream turned horrible nightmare. Sure, the sex was mind blowing and certainly the best birthday present ever, but really, did it have to end with you having a psychotic breakdown?"

Therron quickly walked over to her and pulled her to his strong chest. "Do I feel like a dream? I know this has pushed you to over load right now, but I will explain everything as soon as I handle what happens to be a very serious situation."

He flipped the light switch which plunged the manor into utter darkness. "Just stay where you are, Mandy. I want you be safe and I will come back for you when I have taken care of whatever has to be done. This is urgent, I hate to leave you alone here, but I have to go handle this fast."

He walked in the darkness without a problem and was by his mother's side at the window in seconds. "Where are they now?"

The raven climbed up his arm and onto his shoulder. "One is by the right side of the manor and the other one is behind the barn."

He nodded, then turned with the raven on his shoulder and walked briskly over to the cellar door, leaving Mandy stunned, standing open mouthed against the wall.

Through the darkness, she watched them disappear. She had to get out of here and now! she told herself. Dressed only in the robe, she felt her way through the darkness and into the kitchen. She opened the kitchen door quietly then ran through the rain and into the barn.

Picking up her scattered clothes along the way, she ran towards the Mercedes, hitting her key to start the engine automatically as she continued to run.

Leaping over the convertible's door she landed in the driver's seat with a thud. Putting the car in drive, she turned it sharply and suddenly came face to face with a tall, thin man, who was standing in the middle of the barn. He smiled and his long incisors glistened in the lamp light.

"Get the hell out of my way, Pal or you're toast!" She gunned the car and headed straight for him. Without missing a step, he leaped up and over her car, landing in the backseat. She hit the brakes hard and much to his shock, he went flying forward landing on the front hood.

Smiling, she gunned it again, only this time in reverse. He flew off the hood and landed on his back.

Another eerie looking man, much like the first, appeared at the barn door. He calmly helped his cohort up from the floor and then they both stood and faced her, their smiling faces frightening.

"You can't out run us, witch, so don't even try," the second man told her. Within seconds, he was at her door, reaching in for the keys.

"Goddess and God hear my plea, stop these men from hurting me." With a sweep of her arm, his body flew back against the barn wall and slid to the ground.

The other one charged toward her, while at the same time the cry of a raven could be heard from behind him. Wings wide, the huge bird swooped down, claws drawn and sunk them into the man's skull.

"With these claws I strike you down, becoming one with the ground!" The raven shouted in a high voice.

Mandy watched in disbelief as the man dropped to his knees and slowly disappeared into the barn dirt floor.

"Go now, My Lady, before he arises, Therron will see there are no more surprises." With a flutter of her wings, the raven was gone.

Therron entered the barn at a full run and ground to a halt beside the man Mandy had thrown against the wall. From his belt, he removed a large spike. He held the spike over his head and then drove it into the man's chest.

This must surely be a bad dream," Mandy thought as she wasted no more time before she gunned the Mercedes, leaving the terrifying nightmare behind. She was obviously having one of her famous real to life dreams. She'd awaken safe in her bed, she was sure of it.

Too bad, because Therron Jessie Reyes-Mythos was one hot psychotic trooper. She believed in magic, but a talking raven and a spike welding state trooper—come on, that kind of stuff only happens in the movies.

"Wait!" Therron shouted, as she exited the barn and raced full speed down the driveway. With a push of the button the Mercedes roof eased overhead and blocked out the rain. She turned on the heat, surprised to feel so cold in a nightmare.

Behind her the sky exploded in a flash of fire and noise. Her ears ached from what she was sure must have been the explosion the bird was talking about. She skidded to a stop and looked back. A group of trees to the left of the barn were quickly going up in flames. Luckily it was raining in her dream, so the flames wouldn't last for long.

Hell, maybe this wasn't a dream, and instead, he'd somehow slipped her a drug and she had gotten high?

She hit home on the GPS, and then floored the Mercedes once again, this time without looking back.

All she wanted to do was get home and wake up safe and sound in her own bed. She should have known a hot state trooper wanting her so badly was just a mirage. The least the Goddess of dreams could have done was give her a happy ending on the eve—she glanced at the car's dashboard clock, then said out loud, "Ah hell, on the morning of my half century, old crone, old fart, old maid, birthday!"

FOURTEEN

This could not be happening! He'd scared the only woman he truly loved away. It had been so easy to go back to the way things had been with her, so easy in fact that he had forgotten that she didn't remember him at all.

Instead of going slow, he'd managed to make a mess of everything by revealing himself as a crazy psycho killer, whose mother happened to be a talking raven.

From the corner of his eye, he saw the second vampire's form reemerging from the dirt floor. Peeling a spike off his belt, he walked angrily over to him, and without a second thought, skewered him with it.

Therron, the great hunter, dropped to his knees and began to weep uncontrollably. Soft wings alighted on his shoulder.

"Easy my son, all will be well."

"Be well, Mother? Really? The woman I love thinks I'm a nut job and as we speak, she is fleeing from me, and you tell me all will be well?" He wiped the tears away and slowly stood up, letting his mother adjust to the change in posture.

"Cackle...cackle...cackle."Lady Raven flittered around on his shoulder, then his head.

"You think this is funny, Mother?"

"My son, you do remember that I am one of the most powerful witches in the world?" She flew off his head and landed on the top of a stall door. From where he stood it looked to him like she was posing proudly.

Therron rolled his eyes. "Sorry, that's a little hard to do since you've been in the form of a raven for, oh, I don't know... a few hundred years!"

Flapping her winds angrily, she pecked at the wood with her long, sharp beak. "Do not speak to me in such a demeaning way, My son or I will be forced to show you just how powerful I really am."

Therron shook his head. "The only way I'd believe you were a powerful witch is for you to somehow get Mandy to come back through that door and into my arms."

Flapping her wings, she alighted and landed several times in frustration. "Ah, but you see, my son, I've done something even better than that."

He walked over to his mother and stood nose to beak with her. "What is that supposed to mean, Mother?"

"I've given you a complete um...." She paced back and forth, her sleek black head moving side to side.

"A complete what, Mother?" Therron frowned as he waited for his mother to find the right words.

"Shush, Therron. Sometimes, being a witch of a few hundred years old, I have difficulty remembering modern terms. It is so difficult to stay with all the different terms and tangled up words that don't mean what they did a mere few hundred years ago."

Therron coughed and raised his eyebrows skeptically.

"A lady never tells her real age son, Now, as I was saying, I've given you a complete...I have made her forget..." she pecked the wood in real irritation, and then hopped up so suddenly Therron jumped. "Do-over! Yes! That's it, a do-over!"

"A do-over?" Therron held out his arm and Lady Raven alighted from the stall door. "Ah, a do-over. Brilliant!"

She landed on his arm, keeping her giant claws folded so as not to hurt him. "Your witch is going to wake up in her warm bed a few hours from now believing this was a dream given to her by the Goddess."

He smiled at his mother. "Have I told you lately how much I love you? Sorry about the raven remark." He said as he caressed her feathered head. "I know how hard it must be for you and I promise you that we will find a way to reverse the curse, Mom."

She nibbled his ear and whispered. "I love you too, Son."

Together the strange pair made their way through the rain and into the warm safety of Raven's Hood.

FIFTEEN

Incessant knocking woke her from a sound sleep at 7:00 am in the morning. She sat up with a start, patting the bed with delight. "It really was a dream! Oh, thank you Goddess!"

Not waiting for an invitation, the door opened and Kit Montague burst through singing, "Happy Birthday to you! Happy Birthday to you! Happy Birthday to my wonderful, amazing, sexy, vibrant friend, Mandy! Happy Birthday to you!!!"

She hurled herself onto the bed and landed right next to Mandy. "So how is the birthday girl? Did you have fun last night?"

"Um, yeah. Thanks for throwing me such a nice party."

Kit leaned back while staring down at her friend. "Don't you dare hold out on me missy! I'm your best friend and I want all the juicy details!"

Just outside the window a lone crow caw sounded.

Kit and Mandy's eyes suddenly went blank along with all their memory of last night's events. They both blinked a few times in confusion.

"You want some breakfast?" Kit asked groggily.

"Yes, please," Mandy said softly. She eased her legs off the bed and reached for her robe on the chair. "What were you just saying?

Kit shook her head. "Darned if I can remember." She rubbed Mandy's arm. "Come on birthday girl, you have a big day ahead of you!"

The girls headed downstairs and if anyone ever thought a raven couldn't smile, one look outside Mandy's window at Lady Raven perched smugly on a branch would change that belief.

With a flutter of her beautiful black wings, Lady Raven was gone.

The rest of the day was spent celebrating Mandy's birthday. Her friends gathered around her and by the end of the day she was happily content. The dream crossed her mind occasionally with regret that the mind blowing sex part hadn't been real.

However, the dull ache between her legs made her second guess it being a dream from time to time.

At 9 o'clock she climbed into her bed and slipped beneath her soft, warm covers and fell fast asleep, Windy and Hood snored next to her. Five o'clock would come too soon and tomorrow it was back to work as a paramedic, with Kit as her partner.

The curtains ruffled against the breeze coming through the open window. From the tree top next to the house Therron looked in longingly at the one woman who had captured his heart. With any luck he'd win it back again tonight.

With a flash of his cape he disappeared.

SIXTEEN

Mandy's subconscious woke her abruptly, as a sensation of being watched assailed her senses. Without moving a muscle, she honed her mind to discover the invader. He stood in the corner, tall, dark, and handsome as hell. Strangely, the dogs remained asleep. She rose naked from the bed and slowly walked to him.

He stared at her, his eyes devouring her sexy body. He reached out and pulled her into his rock hard chest. Firm lips found hers and he kissed her deeply, flicking his tongue in and out.

Lowering his hands to her breasts, he cupped them, playing with their nipples. Arching her back, she brought her breasts closer to his sexy mouth.

He smiled at his wanton witch as he latched onto her pert nipple—suckling, licking. Moaning, she shifted her body, pulling his head down with her hand.

Dropping to the floor, he balanced himself on his knees and grasped her hips, pulling her love triangle to his waiting tongue. Spreading her moist lips with his fingers he arched her backwards, jamming his tongue inside her.

Overcome with sexual excitement, she pushed down on his shoulders, sending him gently onto his back. With her sharp nails, she flicked off his shirt buttons, one at a time. Pulling open the black shirt, she lowered her mouth onto his nipple, suckling, teasing him with her tongue. Moaning with delight, he slowly lowered the zipper on his pants and pushed them down. Naked and hard as a rock, he flipped her around until her moist box was on his face and her mouth was sucking his rod.

Tongues, hands, mouths, lips licked and felt their way to wild abandonment. Just as he came in her mouth she twisted around, lying down on his hot body, rubbing her love button on his hardness.

Kissing his juices off her lips, he pulled her butt apart and tickled the hole with his fingers, driving her mad with desire.

She eased herself up so that his shaft, already hard again, tantalized the opening of her sex canal. Teasing, dipping just enough to make him think his was going in for a hard landing.

Slowly he pushed his finger inside her butt hole and with his other hand pushed her body down, impaling her on his swollen shaft.

Eyes hooded and glazed over with passion met his as she thrust and grinded her body on his. He kept his load in until her breathing got fast and shallow and she came with a loud moan. His rod fired off, spilling his seed inside of her, filling her love canal.

She was his, now and forever. Pulling out, he rolled behind her and drew her into his embrace. Kissing her neck, he spooned for the first time in years. Sure, he'd had lovers since she'd disappeared, but never did he remain with them or let them stay in his bed. They were for release and release only and he had cared for them, but he never loved them. This woman was his one love, and somehow he had to make her understand that. His mom had done some kind of memory erase spell, but he wanted her to remember their love making.

Outside, the sun had begun to preview light shadows on the horizon heralding a new day. Therron kissed her head lovingly and then disappeared.

The alarm blared out a tune at 05:15 in the morning as Mandy rolled over and hit the dismiss button. Like a movie, she replayed the vivid dream she'd just awoken from. "What a dream," she whispered "Why couldn't a guy like that be real and actually show up in my bed?" Stretching, she realized that she felt even more sore than yesterday—if that was possible. Her clit felt swollen and tingly and her insides raw.

As a powerful witch, she knew that her mind may be spelled or bewitched, but her body could never hide the true facts. She'd had sex, no two ways about it.

Did she get drunk at the party and hook up? No way, she'd been in bed by 9:00 last night. Thankfully, she and her best friend Kit were working together today, she would help her figure this out.

After showering and doing her makeup, she slipped on her uniform and went downstairs. Kit, also in uniform, was in the kitchen pouring two cups of chai tea.

Looking up, she said, "Wow, something is different about you this morning, Mandy. There's an actual glow about you?"

Mandy walked over to the hallway mirror and looked at her reflection. Her skin glowed softly—she looked young and vibrant. What was going on?

"I think I had sex with a hot guy last night," she remarked.

"You went to bed at 9:00 last night. What'd you do, get up and go out to meet someone?" Kit handed her the tea with eyebrows raised. "I didn't hear you go out or anyone come in, and the alarm was still on when I woke up this morning."

Mandy sat down and sipped her tea. "I can't explain it, Kit. Something happened to me yesterday and last night. My mind may not remember, but my body certainly does," she said, rubbing her forehead in confusion.

Kit pat her friend's back as she sat at the table." Is there a spell to counter act something like this?" Mandy said.

"It's almost time to leave," she continued, "I'll get the book of shadows and bring it with us so we can check if there is such a spell. If anyone can help me figure this out, it's you." Mandy stood up and hugged her friend who hugged her back.

"Mind if I drive?" Mandy said, walking out of the kitchen into the family room. She stopped at the desk. "It will keep my mind from stewing on the way to work."

"Sure, I'll be glad to play Miss Daisy today." Kit picked up her coat and slipped it on. "Looks like rain this morning with clearing later on. Hopefully no wrecks until the sky's clear so we can fly them out on the medevac chopper."

Mandy unlocked the desk drawer and pulled out the book of shadows. She placed it inside her duffle bag and scooped up the keys for the Mercedes SUV. "What else needs to be done for the sleeping beauties?" She gazed lovingly around the family room where a herd of slumbering greyhounds lay, snoring happily.

"Nothing, I fed them and let them out, so we're good to go." Kit lifted her backpack onto her shoulder.

"Sorry I didn't come down to help." Mandy grimaced. "I think I was otherwise occupied."

Kit winked. "Looks like our wish for you came true, even if you can't remember it." Laughing, she opened the door and walked out to the garage.

Mandy followed, shutting the door quietly so as not to disturb the dogs, then locked it behind her.

SEVENTEEN

Earlier that morning, he'd found his mother in the kitchen. "You did what?" he snarled at the raven who paced back and forth along the counter.

"I thought you wanted her to forget what happened son, so I put a mild amnesia spell on her. It was only a little, itsy bitsy, simple spell, not a difficult task for someone with my knowledge." Lady Raven fluffed out her wings. "It won't hurt her, so what is your problem?"

He came at her, nose to beak. "My problem is that am in I love with her, Mother. I don't want her to forget me! Now I have to try and figure out how the hell I'm going to us get back to where we were, before you stuck your beak where it doesn't belong."

"Love has a way of breaking through a spell such as the tiny, miniscule one I cast on her," she told him with a total lack of concern for his annoyance with her. "Perhaps you should make a short visit to her before she wakes up." She peeked up at him with her little black bird eyes, "That might be a really, really good idea."

So, he'd taken his mother's advice and gone to Mandy and he had wooed her with every ounce of lust and love he felt for her. He hoped with all his heart that it had worked.

It was almost 5:30 in the morning by the time he arrived home to shower and change into his uniform. Today he'd be flying the friendly skies as one of the pilots for Sky Angels Inc. Piloting the medevac helicopter was his true passion.

Tucking his pants into his boots, he adjusted them to blouse over top in the favored combat style. At least today he'd be out of sight from the troopers, who lived to bust his chops.

Running late, he grabbed a quick cup of coffee before heading out the door. He'd be there in two minutes if he could use his other worldly skills, but then how could he explain where his car was? Thankfully the hanger wasn't too far from his house so he'd make it in the nick of time.

Therron noticed that the weather wasn't cooperating for any job that required flying this morning, but hopefully, by afternoon, it would be a clear go. There was nothing better than guiding the massive chopper into a narrow landing zone and getting a critically injured or ill patient safely to the hospital in record time.

He was convinced part of the reason the troopers at his barracks disliked him was because of his pilot's status. They only wished they could do what he was able to do.

Gunning the engine, he shot down the long driveway and onto the highway. Mandy had been amazing this morning and instead of his lust for her being sated, it seemed that it grew with each passing minute. Not just lust, but genuine all-encompassing love.

They'd met a few hundred years ago. Then Mandy had been in her first human form; a saucy redhead with swinging hips and a laugh that always made his heart sing. He'd fallen madly in love with her. The night they'd come for her, claiming her to be a witch, he'd been out drinking with the boys at the pub. He'd failed her and never forgiven himself. She'd been executed before he could even get to the magistrate to plead her case. His love, his lass gone from him for that lifetime and as it turned out, several human life times more.

Relaxing to the purr of the engine, he smiled, thinking about the second chance they'd been given. Mandy obviously had no recollection of her previous life, or him, so he was going to have to work to win her heart again.

Rounding a sharp turn in the road, he slowed to avoid hydroplaning. Glancing at the clock, he only had five minutes to get to the hanger, which luckily, was just down at the end of the road. Pulling into the airport, he angled the car into a parking space, got out and practically ran into the office.

This was the one place he was truly accepted. The other pilots respected him and he called a few of them genuine friends. He hoped to be doing this job full time by the end of the year.

Until then, he was only called for sick outs, vacation coverage or open shifts.

"Yo, minute man!" Pilot Henry Fresco called out as he walked through the door at 6:59 am.

"Sorry Fresco, I had a hot date last night and didn't get home until 5:30 this morning."

Fresco patted him on the back. "Man, you change girlfriends like I change socks!" Laughing, Fresco handed him a fresh cup of coffee. "Do tell. Since I got divorced last year and swore off women, I have to live vicariously through you."

"I hate to tell you, but your living vicariously through me is going to stop, if I have anything to say about it."

Fresco leaned back, eyebrows raised and grinned. "So this is the one? I never thought I'd see the day that Mr. Tall, Dark and Handsome settled down!"

Jessie winked. "Let's go check out the ship and I'll tell you all about her."

Together the two handsome pilots strode outside and then into the hanger where the BK117 awaited. The chopper had been christened Falcon 1.

Like a finely tuned team the two men went to work inspecting the ship and making sure that it was ready to go on the next emergency flight.

EIGHTEEN

Mandy drove silently, twisted up in knots over the fact that she was slowly, but surely losing her mind! She was too young for dementia, right?

Kit reached over the console and squeezed Mandy's hand. "You okay?"

Mandy shook her head as a silent tear drifted down her cheek. "I think I am going crazy, Kit."

Kit opened the Book of Shadows and tapped on a page. "I don't think so, my friend. I mean, if you didn't have the physical sensations and signs of.... um..."

"Having had hot, wild sex—yes, go ahead, you can say it." Mandy squirmed in her seat as raw desire shot through her sore sex center.

"Okay then, so if you didn't have all the signs pointing to the fact that you had hot, wild sex with an unknown man, I'd be tempted to think you indeed are losing your mind. But you do have all the symptoms that would go with you having a wild night as a sex object." Kit gave a little laugh.

Mandy snorted. "Gee, thanks partner."

Kit tapped the page and then she ran her pointer finger down the text. "Here it is—I've found a spell that gives its lucky recipients amnesia. It can't, however, block any physical sensations."

Mandy nodded as she turned the Mercedes into the parking lot of the two hundred year old Franklin Hospital. She slowly made her way to the paramedic headquarters, located on the lower level of the beautiful old building that was said to be nearly 200 years old.

The hospital had a lot of rich history and some colorful ghosts still hanging around long after their expiration date. It was rumored that if you stood on the roof of the hospital you could see the Delaware Water Gap located many miles away.

Once Mandy found a good parking spot, she leaned over the console and read the spell Kit had located. "Wow, that's exactly what this feels like. Who would have, or for that matter, who could have, put that spell on me?"

After exchanging a look of confusion, the two medics got out of the car, still shaking their heads in bewilderment. As they headed towards the entrance, deep in conversation, the night crew suddenly came barreling out the door, nearly knocking them both down.

"You got a job?" Mandy said, jumping out of their way.

"Yeah, imminent delivery in Sparta." The medic handed Mandy his keys and radio. "Glad you gals are here. I hate delivering kids!"

Kit grabbed the keys and radio from the other member of the night crew and followed Mandy to the Suburban known as Medic 31.

Without the time to bring their lunch bags, knap sacks and computers in the building, they put them on the back seat of the emergency equipped vehicle.

Mandy clipped her bat girl belt around her waist and dropped her portable radio in the usual pocket. She then slipped behind the wheel of 31 and watched as Kit quickly put on her equipment before jumping in the Suburban.

At the same time that the engine roared to life, Kit picked up the mic. "Medic 31 to Sparta, we're coming to you, ETA approximately seven minutes."

"Copy. Officers requesting you step it up. Patient is in the lobby of the police department in active labor."

Kit and Mandy looked at each other grimacing. "Received Sparta," Kit said.

Mandy flipped on the overhead emergency lights and the windshield wipers, then gunned the truck out of the garage. It was a dreary gray day with a warm mist falling. The Sparta Police Department wasn't too far away and the traffic was light. They made great time and pulled into the parking lot just six minutes later.

Officer Smith met them at the door. He grabbed their bags and pointed them to the lobby.

Lying on the floor of the police station lobby, the female patient was supine on several blankets. Just as Kit and Mandy approached, the woman withered in pain as a full contraction took over her body.

Nothing brought out more responders, and anxiety than a baby delivery. Mandy quickly double gloved and put on a protective gown.

Kit tore open the maternity kit and handed the items to Mandy who was now kneeling at ground zero.

Kit quickly pulled on gloves and knelt down by the side of the patient.

"My name is Mandy, and this is my partner Kit. What's your name?"

The woman gritted her teeth, sweat dripping down her face and chest. "Lily. Fuck! This hurts!"

Mandy nodded. "Okay everyone, I need you to form a circle, facing out, so Lily has some privacy. If you aren't a member of emergency services you need to leave! Except for you." She pointed to a man who looked ready to faint; she figured he was the dad to be. "You get yourself up to your wife's head and help her breath."

"Did you take Lamaze?" Kit questioned.

He nodded then grimaced as Lily squeezed his hand with what seemed like super-human strength, during another contraction.

"Is this your first baby?" Kit asked.

"First and last!" yelled Lily with feeling.

"When's your due date?"

"It was last week. The contractions started this morning and the doctor said we should wait until they get to be just a few minutes apart before going to the hospital. Everyone I spoke to swore that with first baby the labor is always long!"

"We've delivered a whole bunch of healthy babies between us so don't you worry—everything's going to be fine," Mandy told her. She looked at Kit and the father to be and smiled in excitement. "Get ready for delivery."

Mandy pulled down Lily's pants and undergarments and shimmied sterile pads underneath her." Contractions are a minute a part. Okay, everyone let's have this baby!" Mandy smiled.

Kit picked up the bulb syringe and stood ready.

"Okay Lily, your baby's head is showing already, so this is gonna be quick. When the next contraction hits, I want you to push with everything you've got."

Lily nodded then looked up at her husband with a sneer. "You did this to me!"

Mandy and Kit smiled shaking their heads.

"Hey Dad, don't worry, Lily's just hit something called transition. Until the baby is delivered, you just sit there and take it!" Mandy knew the next contraction was coming soon and stayed ready to catch the baby.

Lily started breathing fast. "Oh my God, it's coming—I can feel it coming!" The contraction slammed into her belly like a freight train.

"Okay Lily, let's have your baby. Push!" Mandy placed her gloved hands on the babies crowning head and gently guided it out of the birth canal."

With the head out, but not the shoulders, Kit quickly suctioned the babies nose and mouth to clear out any merconium or liquid so that the new born could take its' first breath safely.

Slowly the tiny shoulders emerged, first the right one and then the left. "Lily, I don't want you to push too hard and tear. Just keep breathing nice and easy, your baby's doing just fine."

Within the next few seconds Mandy was holding a brand new perfect baby boy. "Congratulations Mom and Dad you have a wonderful baby boy!"

Kit dried the baby off and then held out a clean towel and sheet which Mandy used to carefully wrap around him.

"Dad, do you want to cut the cord?" Kit said, holding out a pair of EMS shears toward him.

Overcome with emotion he nodded taking the shears from her. "Yes and thank you both."

"I've clammed off both sides of the umbilical cord. One on the baby's side and one on Lily's side. You must cut in the middle of the two clamps. Got it?" Kit asked.

"Yes, I got it." Dad knelt down beside the two paramedics and cut the cord between the clamps.

Suddenly the foyer was filled with the sound of all the emergency responders clapping with mingled relief and joy at the birth of the new baby. This type of emergency call was one of the few happy ones that the crews ever got to experience.

The baby, now separated from his mother, suddenly let out a cry of all cries. Mandy slowly lowered him onto Lily's chest. "He's just beautiful. Does he have a name yet?"

Lily hugged her new son to her and with her other arm reached out for her husband seeming to have already forgotten the pain she had suffered. He gently took her hand and bent down to kiss her. "You were great, my wife."

"You were pretty great yourself, my husband. I love you so much."

Kit once again knelt next to Mandy who was changing her gloves. "Any sign of the placenta?"

"No, and I hope it gets here soon, I need something cold to drink. I'm already sweating up a storm and the shift just started." She examined Lily for abnormal bleeding or clots, seeing none, she let herself relax, happy to see there was no sign of hemorrhaging.

"Lily, we are going to wait a few minutes for the placenta to deliver. It is very important that all of it gets released so your uterus is clear. Let us know when you start to get contractions again, okay?"

Lily nodded, while she happily cooed her baby.

Several minutes later, Lily grunted. "I'm starting to have one."

Kit positioned herself to examine Lily. "Okay Lily, the placenta is coming, so if you feel the urge to push, go ahead."

With one push the placenta was out and after a quick check by Mandy to be certain it was intact, it was contained in an emesis basin. The placenta would go with Lily to the hospital where the doctors would check it again to make sure it was intact which indicated it had all come out. This was an important step to prevent infection.

"She's all yours, guys." Mandy nodded to the Emergency Medical Technicians.

The EMT's quickly moved in and lifted Lily and baby onto the stretcher. Once she was settled, they wheeled her out to the waiting ambulance.

"You did an awesome job, partner," Kit said.

"You too girlfriend, you too!" Mandy bent down and started cleaning up the bloodied mess of used delivery supplies.

Officer Smith squatted down to help. "You girls were great! Leave that, we'll clean it up." The other cops nodded with happy smiles on their faces, obviously relieved that the medics had showed up so quickly.

"Cool! Thanks fellas!" Mandy picked up the medic bag and walked out to the rig.

Kit followed with the monitor, dodging the rain drops as she made her way to the rig.

Within minutes the ambulance and medic unit were on their way to Newton Hospital with Mom, Dad and brand new baby boy, Arthur on board.

NINETEEN

Lady Raven was stalking across the kitchen counter again, alternately stopping to fluff her feathers or peck the granite with her enormous beak. Once again, she was agitated.

I've really gone and done it this time, she mumbled to herself. As far as her son was concerned, she was sticking her beak where it didn't belong. Well, let him try being cooped up in a bird's body for a few hundred years and see how he liked dealing with the damned feather mites and molting, she continued to mutter to herself as she paced back and forth.

Once she'd been one of the most powerful witches in the entire world. That was until the witch hunts had started and fearing for her safety, her father had turned her into a raven.

Now, he was long since passed and she was still living on as a creature of flight. No matter how much she had studied or tried to find or figure out a spell to reverse what she considered a curse, she had failed.

She lifted her right wing and cleaned the feathers and then her left. She then fluttered them out and fanned the air with both wings spread wide and hovered an inch off the counter top. She actually liked this part of being a bird, it was kind of fun to hover.

She was still a very powerful witch, she acknowledged, as well as a loving mother and unfortunately, still a blasted bird. She hopped over to the small mirror that her son had hung for her and gazed at her shinny beak, those long sleek feathers and then her tiny little eyes. She had to admit the eyes bothered her. She looked forward to the day she could try that stuff the women used on their eyelashes. It made their eyes look so big and wide. She made a guttural noise in her throat as she turned away from her image in disgust.

She hopped over to the sink and spelled the faucet on. Dipping her head beneath the stream of water, she accumulated some water in her beak, then swallowed.

Jumping up onto the faucet handle, she hummed a disco tune she remembered from the late 70's and danced up and down until the faucet shut off. "I have to get my fun wherever I can find it these days," she lamented to the empty room

Done with her morning clean-up routine, she shook out her feathers one final time, then let herself slowly drift off into a meditative state. The answers would come to her this way, she was sure.

Several minutes later, with a beak to tail wiggle, she brought herself to alertness and knew she had figured out a plan. First, she had to go on a scouting party which would help her understand all the circumstances involved so she didn't mess up again. Then she'd repair what needed and somehow, someway, she'd help Therron reclaim the woman of his dreams.

Already, for about the hundredth time today, Lady Raven felt those defeated and depressed feelings come over her about the fact that she was no longer in a woman's body. It was really getting old being a bird. She sighed, then flapping her wings to release all the negative thoughts she's been thinking, she flew straight out the open kitchen window.

TWENTY

It was nearly ten in the morning by the time they had finally finished up with the baby delivery and were back in the truck heading to get breakfast.

They were both on a high after delivering a healthy baby. Lily and Dave, or Dad as he'd been known during the delivery, were both so grateful for their help. There was something so very rewarding about delivering a baby. Birth was always an amazement to watch no matter how many time they witnessed it.

"Where would you like to get something to eat?" Mandy asked Kit.

"How about we head to the bagel place and grab something quick. I'm starving and I want to be sure we get something to eat before we get another job."

"Sounds good," Mandy agreed glancing up at the sky. "At least the weather is clearing." She slipped on her aviators as the sun peeked out from behind the dwindling clouds.

They walked into Firehouse Bagels and quickly ordered. Sitting down, Kit opened the Book of Shadows wide enough so that Mandy could lean over her and read along.

"So it had to be another witch who did this to me. Another witch! This is really freaking me out, Kit."

"It's freaking me out too. Let's call a meeting of the coven for tonight and together we will be able to figure this out. It might not hurt to contact Lady Maveen."

Mandy nodded. "Good idea. I'm going to step out and give her a call now."

Kit scoured the book for any other spells, incantations or herbal mixtures that might have caused Mandy's amnesia. Nothing, but the spell she'd found explained what had happened to her friend.

A few minutes later, Mandy walked back in as white as a ghost. She plopped down next to Kit, who leaned in. "What?"

"Lady Maveen said that because of the spell work we did, my psyche was open and easily influenced by any spells. She agrees with us about the amnesia spell. When I repeated the spell to her, she remembered its origins. A powerful witch named Raven Reyes. She was the High Priestess of the Santigo Coven until she disappeared in the witch hunts."

"Wait a minute. Didn't you say that you think you remember the guy introducing you to a bird and saying it was his mother?"

Mandy grimaced. "Yeah I did, but I feel silly now. I mean, please, that is just too farfetched, even for me to believe."

Kit shook her head. "I wouldn't be so quick to play that down. You told me the troopers name, remember? In case he turned out to be a serial killer."

"I did?" Mandy bit into her bagel. "I don't remember that." She chewed slowly as she shook her head.

"Yes, you did, and his name was, Therron Reyes – Mythos, better known as Jessie."

Recognition coursed through Mandy's body awakening her memory. "Yes, yes, I remember now, you're right, that is his name. So he does exist. I thought I was going crazy."

"You still don't get it do you?" Kit pulled a pen out of her uniform shirt pocket and wrote something down on a napkin."

Therron Reyes - Mythos

Raven Reyes

"See anything now?" Kit bit into her bagel savoring the taste.

"Holy shit! They have the same name. So, what are you saying, that she's his long lost relative?" Mandy took a swig of her hot tea.

"Or mother." Kit finished her bagel and absently crumpled the paper wrap in her hands. "Which would mean that there is something really, really weird going on here. Something supernatural."

Mandy nodded. "I don't even know what to think at this point. But I gotta tell you, I'm just relieved I'm not crazy and that something is going on here that is bigger than I even understand."

Kit opened her mouth to speak but found herself being drowned out by Medic 31 tones.

"Medic 31, respond Route 206 in Montaque for a serious motor vehicle accident. Reported vehicles on fire with entrapment. I'm sending you Medic 51 as back up."

Kit threw her garbage away. "Sounds like a bad one."

Mandy took a last bite of her bagel then threw it in the trash along with her tea. "Good thing we're on this side of the county, we'll be there fast."

The bagel store patrons listened eagerly and watched as the women made their way outside and got in their truck. Several left to follow and watch the action.

The Suburban charged up Route 206 with Mandy at the helm. The lights flashed and the siren screamed as cars pulled over to the side to make way for the emergency vehicle.

"Looks like we've got company." Mandy eased Medic 31 over to the shoulder to let the faster state trooper car pass. Its siren sounded in a quick hello.

Pulling back behind the troop car, she followed letting it lead the way and open a clear path in traffic. Nearly ten minutes later they approached the scene. Flames shot out from the hood of one car which appeared to have struck a large pickup head on. The impact had sent both mangled vehicles flying, each landing at odd angles.

"Holy shit, I hope Medic 51 gets here soon!" Kit picked up the mic. "Medic 31, on scene."

"Which one do you want?" Kit asked.

"I'll take the car." Mandy pulled out the monitor, trauma bag and turn out gear from the back of the medic unit.

"Sounds good." Kit pulled on her heavy, yellow turn out coat and helmet. "You be careful!"

Helmet and coat already on, Mandy picked up the equipment and looked at Kit. "You too, partner. See you at the landing zone."

Feverishly the troopers worked with extinguishers to hold back the flames, until the fire department arrived. Mandy cautiously made her way to the driver's side window and looked in. There was one male occupant who was heavily entrapped by the dash.

A Blue Ridge EMT ran over to her. "What can I do?"

"We need extrication and make sure they have two birds on the way!" The EMT started to turn away. "And get the ETA of the fire truck or we won't need either."

The EMT nodded and ran to his incident command vehicle.

Mandy pulled on the door handle and was amazed to find that despite the heavy damage it opened. She leaned into the car. "Sir, can you hear me?"

His eyes opened slowly, filled with pain. They were blue and reminded her of her dads. His breathing was deep and slow. He locked eyes with Mandy. "Help me."

"We are going to help you. What's your name?" While she talked, she pulled out an IV set up and spiked a 500cc bag of Normal Saline.

"Dan," he whispered.

"Dan, my name is Mandy. We have plenty of help here so try and remain calm; we are going to get you out. I'm going to start an IV on you, okay?" She didn't need vital signs or a heart monitor to tell her the patient was in deep shit.

In the distance she heard the fire engine's sirens. The sound got marvelously closer and closer until they arrived and the wail sounded no more. Just minutes later, heavenly water splashed onto the hood of the car, knocking down the fire. As the last flame went out, she slipped the catheter in, tapped it down and opened the IV wide.

"You still with me Dan?"

He opened those baby blues and smiled weakly. "Once a Marine, always a Marine," he quoted before he closed those amazing eyes again, the strain to keep them open was too much for his weak body.

Next to her, the Jaws of Life roared to life. The fire chief tapped her on the back. "We'll cut him out now paramedic."

She nodded and stepped back, leaving the IV bag secured to seat. Getting the fire fighters attention, she shouted, "Make sure that IV stays in!"

"Will do!" said the chief.

She watched as the Jaws of Life gnashed its way through the mangled steel, slowly, but surely, freeing her patient. It wasn't long before they'd cut away enough to let the EMT's get a backboard in the vehicle and under the patient and finally pull him out.

"Falcon 1 is on the ground at the municipal building," EMT Jan said.

"Fantastic! Let's get him into the bus and get going!" Mandy picked up her equipment and walked over to the ambulance. She turned to where Kit was working on her patient. "Partner, you okay with my going in the first chopper?"

"It's yours!" Kit walked beside her patient who was being wheeled to another ambulance. "Mine is pretty stable. We'll take the second bird."

"Thanks!" Mandy turned back to the rig and threw her equipment in through the open side door. The patient followed through the back double doors.

Mandy pulled on the stretcher and guided into the heavy steel brackets. The stretcher secured into place and she sat down on the bench seat.

"How ya doing Dan?" Pulling out a blood pressure cuff, she wrapped it around the arm closest to her and started squeezing the ball.

His blue eyes opened. "Oh, I've been better."

"Sense of humor intact, I think you're gonna make it." Mandy watched the gauge as it dropped. At 90 she felt his radial pulse. Pulling out another IV, she spiked the bag and hung it from the IV holder in the ambulances ceiling. "Dan, you're a quart low, so I'm going to start another line, okay?"

"Whatever you need to do is fine, but I'm really thirsty, could I have a drink?"

"Sorry, we can't give you anything to drink, Dan. Big pinch," she said as she guided the needle into his vein. All done." She tapped down the line and opened it wide. "We'll be at the landing zone in a few minutes. Then you'll be on your way to the trauma center."

The ambulance made a sharp right turn and wound its way through the hills and curves of Clove Road. It wasn't long before they pulled into the municipal lot and parked a distance away from the white and blue BK117. Shiny silver and blue Falcon emblems were below the rotors on each side.

"How's it going in there? About ready to fly?"said a sexy male voice as the back doors of the ambulance opened.

"One last blood pressure, Dan." Mandy was concentrating so much on the gauge that the words didn't register, but the voice did. She inhaled sharply, not taking her eyes off the gauge. "BP is 110/p and that's pretty good, Dan."

As if watching in slow motion she turned and looked at the 'voice'. Standing in the open doorway stood the most handsome man she'd ever seen. Amber eyes locked onto hers and he smiled.

The flight medic and the nurse eased in beside her and took over Dan's care. Jan gave the flight crew report as she stared at the medic frozen in place.

Slowly, Mandy made her way to the back doors. Therron raised his hand and she took it as if in a trance. His simple assistance out of the ambulance took on a sensual feeling that was ridiculous considering the situation and the amount of people looking on.

She looked up into his eyes. "Hello Mandy," he said huskily.

"I know that I know you, but I can't seem to remember..."

"Ssssh, I promise I will explain, tonight if you'll let me." It took everything he had not to pull her into his arms and kiss her. Behind him his fellow pilot whistled.

Jessie turned around and smiled, waving him over.

"Mandy, this is my co-pilot, Henry Fresco."

"Nice to meet you, Henry."

They moved out of the way as the stretcher carrying the patient exited the ambulance and was then rolled over to the waiting medevac.

"You're a medevac pilot?" Mandy asked perplexed. This was not at all what she was beginning to remember.

"I promise, I'll explain everything later. Can I come to your house at 8:oo tonight?" He took her hand gently in his and lifted it to his lips, kissing it lightly.

Mandy inhaled sharply, and felt her senses explode with remembrance of every sensual episode that had happened between them. Suddenly, memories that had been hidden by the spell, flooded through her and she had to reach out to steady herself.

Therron grabbed her before she fell, and as professionally as possible, helped her over to the ambulance. "You remember me now, don't you?" He motioned for her to sit on the bumper.

Once she was seated and took a few deep breathes, she answered him. "Yes, everything." Her face grew hot as she blushed with embarrassment. "Everything."

"Sweetheart, there is nothing to be embarrassed about. I know you don't understand everything and this will sound real crazy, but I've loved you for so very long and I promise you that I will answer all the questions you have tonight."

She swallowed deeply and nodded.

"I have to go, I'll see you tonight, okay."

"Okay." Mandy watched as Therron strode confidently across the parking lot and got into the waiting chopper.

Kit waited for her patient to be loaded into the second medevac, then practically ran to where Mandy sat quietly on the ambulance's bumper.

Kit knelt down next to her friend and partner. "Are you alright, Mandy?"

"It's him." She pointed to the pilot, sitting on the right side of the ship. "It all happened, everything—it wasn't a dream or a hallucination—it really happened." She looked up into her friend's face, searching for judgment.

Kit squeezed her friend's hand. "Mandy, I will never, ever judge you, you should know that. Honestly, I'm relieved. Plus, the guy is hotter than hell!"

Mandy smiled dreamily. "He is hotter than hell, right?"

"Oh yeah, you are one lucky lady." Kit stepped up into the ambulance and started cleaning up the remnants from the trauma patient.

Mandy followed, briskly reading the trauma bag and monitor for the next call. Her spirits lifted and she felt light and free for the first time since she'd lost her memory.

"You have to admit it's a lot to wrap your mind around, being his mom is a bird and all."

Mandy walked in step with Kit as they carried their equipment back to the medic unit.

Kit nodded as she opened the back door and put the monitor in its slot. "That it is. Judging from how light and happy you suddenly look and feel, I think it's going to be worth whatever it takes to get to the bottom of it all."

Mandy put the trauma bag in its slot, then turned as the rotor blades began to pick up speed. From the cockpit, Therron waved and smiled.

Mandy waved back, then got in the medic truck to watch the bird take off. There is nothing worse than getting hit with flying gravel and other assorted things when a chopper takes off.

Kit joined her. "So when ya gonna see him again?"

"Tonight, if it's okay with you and Frank." Mandy started the engine and positioned Medic 31 so she could get a better view of Therron taking off.

"Of course it's okay. Of course we will discreetly disappear to some as yet unknown destination once you've introduced us." Kit locked her eyes with the handsome pilots. "And if he treats you badly, discreet goes out the window. Kapish?"

Mandy leaned over and hugged her friend. "Kapish. I love you, Sista. Thank you for caring."

Together they watched the blue, white and silver BK117 rise, hover and then take off, flying directly over top of them.

"I love working with you Kit, but I have to say, I can't wait for this shift to be over!" Putting the Suburban in drive, she slowly maneuvered out of the parking lot, carefully parting the watching crowd.

TWENTY ONE

Frank finished putting the last glass in the dishwasher and shut the door soundly. Turning it on, he glanced out the big window over the sink and did a double take.

Outside on the patio the greyhound gang stood in a row. They were staring directly in front of them at a huge raven that was perched on the rock wall that surrounded the area.

Kat moved forward until she was snout to beak with the raven.

Frank didn't know what to do. Should he watch or get out there before someone got hurt? For goodness sake, he was a state trooper wasn't he? Yet, something made him stay rooted in place. All he could do was watch and wait.

On the tan flat rock patio, Kat stepped forward. The large bird had arrived several minutes earlier.

Mind to mind the raven and greyhounds communicated.

"My name is Raven Reyes, High Priestess witch of the Santiago Coven and mother of Therron Reyes-Mythos." She fluffed out her feathers proudly and angled her head away from Kat in respect.

Kat, a medium sized brindle, nodded. "I am Kat, leader of the Greyhound Gang." She turned her snout and touched the first dog with her nose. "Please introduce yourselves."

Kelsey, a small black greyhound with a white chest patch and white paws, stepped forward. "I am Kelsey, I am Kat's sister, and we live here with our human's, Kit and Frank." Backing up, she touched her nose to the greyhound next to her.

A very petite white greyhound stepped forward. "My name is Winter Wonderland, and my human is Kandy Hart, whom I love very much. She adopted me and thus saved my life. If you try to hurt her, I will bite you!" Winter backed up and touched the next dog with her nose.

A huge black greyhound stepped forward and touched his snout to the beak of the raven. "I am Kirby, and I live here with Kat, Kelsey, Kit and my human Frank. If you hurt any of them, you need not worry about the bite Winter Wonderland gives you, because I will eat you." He stepped back and touched the next dog with his nose.

A medium sized tan greyhound stepped forward. "I am Flash, and my human is Connie. I do not live here, but I like it here." He stepped back and touched the nose of the next dog in line.

A huge white greyhound with a brown eye patch stepped forward. "I am Hood, and my human is Mandy and I will defend her always."

He stepped back and touched the side of the last greyhound in line.

A big brindle stepped forward. Normally very sweet, she had a hard edge to her as she stood before the raven. "My name is Wind Shadow. My friends call me Windy, of which you are not one yet. My human is Mandy, and I love her very much. What do you want with us and our humans?" She did not move back.

Kat stepped forward shoulder to shoulder with Windy. "Release our human Frank from your spell or we will eat you!"

Lady Raven fluttered her wings, cawing out loudly. The dogs did not move, and in fact, when she looked again all of them were shoulder to shoulder inches from her.

"I mean no harm to you or your humans. Please hear my plea before I release your human. He is in no pain and is watching. If I release him, he will come out and I will not be able to ask for your help."

Kat huffed. "You have five minutes. You will then release our human Frank, or we will eat you."

Raven jerked her head up and down like she was imitating a pigeon. "Yes, fine. My son, Therron Reyes – Mythos, is in love with your human, Mandy." She jutted her beak at Hood and Wind Shadow. "Your human also loves my son, but she is not aware of it as yet." Raven lowered her feathered head in shame. "This all happened because I put an amnesia spell on her, to protect her."

Hood let out a low and fierce growl. "Remove the spell immediately!"

Frightened of the dog, she quickly hopped up onto a branch. "I have removed the spell, but I do not know if it worked. I want my son and your Mandy to be happy. This is all I most want in this thing you call my life."

"Thank you." Kat walked over to hood and licked his face. "She means what she says Hood. I believe her. Let us hear what she wants of us."

Hood nodded. "I will hear what she says."

"You will not be harmed Raven. Speak your mind," Wind Shadow said softly.

"The spell has been broken, but they need to know. My heart will break if it is not so." Lady Raven fluttered down from the tree and landed on the rock wall. "There is also trouble a foot. Outcast vampires are hunting my son and your human is now involved in this terrible problem. We must work together to keep them safe."

"Release our human Frank and you will have our cooperation," Kat said.

"I release him now, with no ill effects. His day will be good, filled with love as it should. Happy, healthy and abundant is he. So mote it be."

Inside the house Frank shook his head. The fog lifted and he rushed to the kitchen door, out through the mudroom and onto the patio. "What the hell?"

The greyhounds each lay on a chair, sunning themselves as if nothing had taken place. They all looked up at him like he was daffy.

He wasn't sure what was going on, but one thing he knew for sure, was when you lived with a witch, anything was possible. Turning, he walked back into the house and grabbed a beer from the fridge.

TWENTY TWO

"So that's your new lady? I'm happy for you, Jessie. She's gorgeous." Henry clapped him on the back as they waited in the chopper on the roof of Morristown Hospital.

"She's amazing, I'm so lucky. Now, if I can just convince her." He leaned back in the seat and shook his head.

Henry threw back his head laughing. "You, the Romeo of the air are having trouble getting a woman to fall for you? Now that makes my day." He motioned for Jessie to get out.

They stood on the roof as Henry lit a cigarette.

Jessie shook his head. "When are you going to quit those cancer sticks?"

Henry exhaled a large plume of smoke. "Now you sound like my ex-wife." He held up his hand. "I know, I know, I'm going to quit! Okay? Just weaning myself off slowly."

"Heard that before. Geeze, now you're going to stink up the whole ship on the way back." Jessie leaned against the nose of the ship. "Hope we got that guy here in time."

"Me too." Henry threw down the cigarette, half smoked and stomped it out. "Looked like a rough one." He glanced up at the door to the helipad. "Good, here they come. I'm starving.

Let's get this shindig on the road." He climbed back in the left side of the chopper.

"You do mean in the air, right?" Jessie slipped in the right side and started the powerful engine. The rotors started moving slowly at first, then built up speed as the flight paramedic and nurse climbed into the back and buckled into their seats.

Up to speed, Jessie pulled on his head set. "Everybody ready to go?" he said into the mic.

Thumbs up and yes's echoed all around. Jessie released the controls. "You take her Henry. I've got some thinking to do."

Henry smiled and nodded. "Will do stud. Okay if I head to the airport for some chow?"

Thumbs up and oh hell yes's, followed as the ship beat her way into the air and flew away.

TWENTY THREE

"Oh my gosh, will it ever be seven o'clock?" Mandy said watching the clock as though it was a pot of water she was waiting to boil.

"Countdown to hot, wild sex is one hour and fifteen minutes," Kit said, smiling.

"Oh shut up, Dork," Mandy said sarcastically. She looked out the window as she saw a car pull in and park. "One down and one to go, "she said.

Paramedic John Rappaport walked in the door. "Good evening ladies. Anyone got a radio and keys..."

Mandy thrust her radio and keys into his hands.

"Alrighty then, guess someone wants to go home." John pulled out his batman belt and dropped the radio in and then attached the keys to his clip. "Do we need anything in the truck?"

"We had a few calls today, but everything is restocked and ready to go," Kit said.

"Awesome." John sat down at the table. "Might as well stop watching, I'm working with the minute man tonight, remember?"

Mandy let out and exasperated sigh. "Figures, the night I need to get out on time, I have to wait for Mr. 'I'm always late to get here!' If I get a late job, I'm going to blow a bleb!"

Kit let out a snort. "I've got your back. If there's a late job, I'll take it. You go home and I'll hitch a ride with John and Bobby."

John put his feet on the table and leaned back in the chair. "What do you have, a hot date?" he asked sarcastically.

"Yeah, as a matter of fact, she does," Kit said.

His feet dropped to the floor and he leaned forward in the chair. "Wait a minute, after that debacle with the tongue kisser state trooper, I thought you'd sworn off all men." He waited expectantly.

"Well, she's sworn back on," Kit said defensively.

Mandy just stared out the window lost in thought.

John held up his hand. "I didn't mean anything by that, Kit. Just caught me off guard, that's all. You know I think the world of you and Mandy."

"I know you do. Sorry, just want the best for Mandy and I don't want her to get hurt again."

They both looked up to find Mandy staring at them.

"Um, you know I can hear you, right?" She pointed her finger up and down her body. "Yup, standing right here in the same room as you two dweebs."

John laughed. "She's pulling out the big vocabulary now. This guy must be good."

"Oh thank God! Let's go Kit." Mandy picked up her stuff and motioned for her friend to do the same. "Minute man is here."

The two women brushed past the late medic. "Hey, thanks for getting here at start of your shift, as usual!" Mandy spat.

Kit shook her head. "You know we get here early for you!"

Bobby Randal blushed. "Hey I'm sorry. I got stuck in traffic and..."

"My dog ate my stethoscope. Yeah, we've heard it all," Mandy said. She got into the Mercedes, slamming the door and started the engine.

Kit rolled her eyes at Bobby and got into the passenger side. She put her stuff next to Mandy's in the back seat. "Let's go meet your man, partner."

Gunning the engine Mandy drove the Mercedes down the drive and headed towards Serenity Farm. "It won't be long now. I'm excited, and nervous as hell, both at the same time. Thanks for being my friend, Kit."

Kit smiled. "Always, Mandy."

"Oh no! I just realized that I never gave him the address to Serenity Farm! How is he going to find me? He doesn't have my phone number either. Oh no!" Her shoulders sagged and she took her foot off the gas.

"What!" Kit said.

"No, it's true. I was so caught up in finding out that he was real, that I didn't even think. Oh, Kit."

Kit leaned over and rubbed Mandy's shoulder. "Sometimes we just have to trust that the Goddess and God make things happen that we can't see in the real world. Time to trust."

Mandy nodded, pressing down on the gas, she headed to Frankford, NJ.

TWENTY FOUR

"Good luck tonight, Jessie." Henry clapped his fellow pilot on the back.

"Thanks buddy."

Therron picked up his brief case and headed out the door to his black Camaro. Slipping behind the wheel, he put his brief case on the front seat next to him and started the car. It was now or never.

Putting the address of Serenity Farm into the GPS, it hit him that he'd never asked her for it. One more thing to explain.

He'd showered, shaved, put on sexy cologne and changed into jeans and tight white tee shirt, before leaving Sky Angels HQ.

It would take him just about forty-five minutes to get there and it was nearly 7:15 already.

He floored the new muscle car and raced towards his girl. His girl—that sounded so good to him. He had so much to explain. He just hoped somehow that she would be able to remember, and to understand everything he was going to tell her.

She was either going to fall into his arms and love him, or reject him and call him a looney toon. It wasn't easy being a vampire hunter and healer. Yet he'd waited several life times to find her again. He wasn't going to give up until she loved him as much as he loved her.

His soul mate awaited.

Therron didn't see them lurking next to the hanger as he pulled away. If he had, he'd never have left his friend Henry Fresco and the relief pilots there alone.

TWENTY FIVE

Mandy had showered, changed and beautified herself, trusting as Kit had said, that the Goddess and God would come through.

She sat in the kitchen sipping on fresh brew iced tea along with Kit and Frank.

Kat, Kelsey, Kirby, Windy and Hood gnawed on their natural bones, sensing that something big was afoot.

The clock was exactly 7:59 when they all froze at the sound of the engine of a muscle car approaching.

"He's here." Mandy set down her tea.

"What do you want us to do?" Frank asked.

"Just act normal." Mandy stood up, her whole body shaking. "You know, normal like we always are."

"Do you always shake like a wet Chihuahua?" asked Frank. His question was answered with a smack to his arm by Kit. "Ouch!"

"Honey, just take deep meditative breaths." Kit suggested, then paused before starting to speak again.

"Center yourself and all will be well. Of this I know, of this I can tell. You and your man will heal all wounds and come to know the truth very soon. Love will conquer all your woes and Therron Jessie Reyes-Mythos will be your beau. So mote it be."

Mandy smiled. "Did you just spell me?"

Kit shrugged her shoulders. "Maybe." Smiling, she hugged her friend just as the doorbell rang. "Now go get 'em tigress."

Mandy felt the confidence spell soar through her as she walked to the door. The patter of greyhound feet could be heard as the dogs followed her. They were all turning the corner at the exact moment that she opened the door.

Therron stepped inside, smiling but in the next moment his mouth opened in surprise and his eyes grew as big as saucers.

The moment that Mandy had been waiting for all day—that romantic kiss and hug that she had dreamed of, became instead, a gaggle of greyhounds jumping on Therron, while Kit and Frank did their best to get them under control.

Grabbing Kirby's collar, Frank extended his hand to Therron. "Hi, I'm Frank. Mandy said to act normal, so ready or not, here we are."

Mandy smacked him in the upper arm.

"Ouch!" Frank smiled, pulling Kirby, and then Kat, into the family room.

Kit extended her free hand, which Therron grasped in a strong hand shake. "Nice to see you again and yup, Frank's right, this is our normal." She pointed to Mandy's dogs. "I think these two need an introduction before going to doggie jail." Kit guided Kelsey away and into the family room.

Therron shook his head, laughing. "Well Ms. Devine, you certainly are unique." He knelt down by the brindle and the white and brown greyhounds and held out his hand for them to sniff.

Mandy knelt down next to him. She reached out and pet the big brindle dog. "This is Wind Shadow or Windy as her friends call her.

"Well hello, Wind Shadow, may I call you Windy?"

Windy nodded and sneezed bumping his hand with her wet nose.

Mandy reached out to the white and brown dog and pat him on his back. "This is Hood."

"Hello Hood, nice to meet you. Is it okay if I get to know your mom?

Hood bumped his head into his hand and huffed. Licking Therron's hand, he then bumped his nose on Windy's side and they both walked into the family room.

Therron stood and held out his hands for Mandy to grasp. Pulling her up, he wrapped his arms around her and pulled her into his broad chest. "Hello, Mandy," he said in his all too sexy voice and then she finally had the welcome she been dreaming of.

She felt his power course through her body as she stood on bare feet tippy toed and kissed him. "Hello Therron Jessie Reyes - Mythos."

"My friends call me Jessie." He kissed her back deeply, sensually.

"Then, hello Therron, for I intend to be so much more than just your friend." Brazenly, she ran her hands down his back and cupped his tight jean covered ass.

Surprise lit his face as he inhaled deeply. "We have so much to talk about. I need you to understand who I am and who we once were..."

"Sssssh, shut up and kiss me." Mandy grabbed his thick dark hair and pulled his mouth back down to hers. "I love the way you kiss. You taste like fresh mint tea on a summer afternoon."

"I can't keep my hands off you, my little witch."

She grabbed his hand pulling him up the stairs. "Good night Kit, Frank and Greyhound Gang."

Now it was his turn to blush. "Mandy I just got here. I mean, is this normal?"

She stopped mid-step on the staircase. "Oh honey, this is anything, but normal, which is exactly why they won't say a word. They want me to be happy and I haven't been this interested or excited about anyone in a very long, long time."

"In that case, what are we doing standing on this stair case?" He kissed her once more before he felt her hand grasp his and pull him onward.

Opening the door to the room named Yellow Cottage, she backed into the huge living area, kissing Therron as she grabbed onto his shirt yanking it over his head.

He shut the door with a push of his cowboy boot and followed his witch to her bed. She was a wild child in this life and he was loving every minute of it.

They fell together onto her king size bed, he on top of her. She wrapped her legs around him and grinded against the bulge in his tight blue jeans.

An all-encompassing passion, not of this world, enveloped them as they removed each other's clothes with wild abandonment.

Finally naked they continued kissing.

He ran his hands up and down her toned body, cupping her breasts, which fit perfectly in his hands. Her body was no longer that of a twenty year old which was perfect for him. He explored every inch of her with his hands, tongue and hard on.

"Where?" he growled.

"Top drawer," she whispered, caught up in wild, hot sexual desire.

He reached in and pulled out lube and a condom. Gently he rubbed heated liquid over her triangle and sex tunnel. Kissing her he slowly slipped the condom over his rock-hard shaft.

Locking eyes with her, he calmed the animal passion and replaced it with soul passion. He pushed his shaft into her warm, moist tunnel, slowly.

Her eyes looked back at him with matching passion as she wrapped her legs around him again and felt him fill her.

They moved as one, staring deeply into each other's eyes, feeling love as deep as the sands of time.

Passion built like a slow moving train, until it burst forth onto the track like a screaming bullet locomotive.

He pounded into her, rubbing against her mound. Deep inside her, waves of pleasure built and built one on top of another until they burst forth in a mother of all orgasms. "Therron!"

He drove his member in once more, and then came like the rush of the ocean. "Mandy, oh my beautiful, incredible, Mandy. I love you baby, I love you so much, never leave me—never again."

"I know that you're my soul mate, Therron. You are now as you have been in the past, as you will be in the future. I love you too."

They fell asleep naked and entwined as one. Tomorrow would bring the dawn and questions to answer. For now, they had each other and nothing else mattered.

TWENTY SIX

The three pilots, along with the two remaining flight medics and the nurse had been easy marks. Not only would Therron be going down in flames, but all his little friends were going along with him!

The two Outcast vampires lugged the sedated and restrained flight crew outside and tossed them into an idling black van.

Now for the fun part. The three Outcasts grabbed their tools and ambled over to the vulnerable aircraft, Falcon 1.

Like a well-practiced team, they went about all the necessary tactics to sabotage the lifesaving emergency helicopter.

Tomorrow, Therron would get a call to come in and replace the missing pilots. Then they would place a fake call, claiming an emergency and then Therron and crew would be history.

They finished packing up all the evidence that they had made adjustment to the aircraft and headed back to the van. The hostages, or rather dinner, as the Outcasts thought of them, lay prostrate in the back. The sedative wouldn't wear off for hours.

Settled in the still idling van, they slowly made their way out of the lot, gravel crackling under its wheels.

TWENTY SEVEN

Therron woke up with a start at 4:00 am. Something was wrong - very, very wrong!

Looking at his love lying peacefully next to him, he quietly eased out from under the covers and got dressed.

His phone glowed from the bedside table showing multiple missed calls and voice mails.

Walking to the side of the bed where, Mandy lay asleep, he bent down and kissed her lightly on the top of her head. "I love you, Mandy," he whispered lovingly, "and no matter what the day ahead brings, please remember that."

With a whoosh, he left the room and appeared at his car. He got in and put his phone in the cradle. Hitting send, he listened as his boss frantically told him the crew members were missing, among them, his friend Henry.

Once he'd finished listening to his voice mail, he dialed his boss who answered before the first ring ended.

Therron couldn't believe what he was hearing, it sounded too unbelievable. Something must have happened shortly after he'd left!

Starting the engine, he slowly made his way down the driveway, hoping not to wake anyone who was still sleeping inside the mansion.

He missed seeing the curtain fall back down, covering the face of Frank, who had been watching from the window.

Leaving behind Serenity Farm, he rushed to Sky Angels Inc. headquarters. He pulled into the lot forty minutes later.

The place was crawling with cops and FBI agents. Matt Shane, who was his boss, met him by his car. "It's bad Jessie, real bad."

Therron got out of his car and stood next to his boss and friend. "What the hell happened? How can an entire flight crew and Henry simply disappear?"

"I don't know how or why it happened. We didn't find out until there was a call that came in for Falcon 1. It wasn't until then that we figured out something was wrong. When they didn't answer, after repeated requests, the cops were sent here to check on them. When they arrived the ship was here, but not one member of the crew. All their things are here though—it's like they all just went poof." He shook his head and began to pace.

"I'm going to check in with the investigators and take a look around, maybe being a pilot I will spot something out of the norm that they wouldn't pick up on." Therron pat his boss on the shoulder and walked away, heading to the hanger where command center was set up.

He held out his hand for the FBI agent, obviously in charge. "Hi, I'm Trooper Jessie Reyes

- Mythos and I work here part time as a pilot. How can I help?"

"Thanks, I'm special agent Aldo Storms," the investigator informed him and shook his hand soundly. "Welcome aboard. Any help you can give us will be greatly appreciated. When was the last time you were here, or saw any of the missing persons?"

"I was here yesterday with one of the missing pilots, Henry Fresco. I can't understand what could have happened? Do you have any leads?"

"Nothing, absolutely nothing. There are no signs of a struggle, and all of their belongings are here, undisturbed. We've been waiting for a ransom call, but so far nada. Where were you last night?"

Therron didn't take offense to the question, he knew the special agent was just doing his job. "I was with my girlfriend, Mandy Devine, at her house. I left there as soon as I got the messages from my boss that they were missing."

"Okay, just so you know, we are going to verify that."

"No problem, I understand fully. Mind if I take a look around?" Therron asked.

"Help yourself. The scene has already been processed, so don't worry about destroying any evidence."

Therron walked through the scene looking for anything out of place. He'd almost gone through the entire scene when he smelled it. The scent of an Outsider. He sniffed the air letting it lead him to a rag in the corner of the hanger. "Damn it." he thought to himself, "I should have known those ass holes just never give up. It's one thing to go after me, that's expected. It is a whole other thing to go after my friends!"

Suddenly in the sky a raven appeared. It headed directly to Falcon 1, landing on the tail. Therron slowly walked over to the rear of the ship.

"Mother what are you doing here?" he hissed, pretending to examine the rear rotor as he stared his mother in the eyes.

Raven fluffed her feathers. "I sensed something was wrong, so I came right away. I am happy you are safe, my son."

He relaxed, recognizing that his mother was worried about him. "I'm okay, Mom. My friends, however, are all missing. Do you have any ideas about where we can find them?"

She paced back and forth on the metal tail. "Get me something that belongs to one of them who is closest to you and meet me back at Raven's Hood Manor. I have just the spell in mind."

He nodded, and then made a grand gesture of shooing the bird off the medevac helicopter. "Go on! Get out of here bird!"

The raven took off flying so low the FBI agents all ducked.

Therron walked over to the special agent in charge. "I'm sorry sir, I just don't see anything out of the ordinary in here. Mind if I check out the crew room?"

The special agent nodded toward the crew room. "Knock yourself out trooper." He turned back to his paperwork.

Therron knew just the thing he was going to get, Henry's brush. The guy loved his hair and was always checking himself out in the mirror or brushing his blonde hair.

He nodded at an FBI agent coming out of the crew room. The guy paused about to detain him until the special agent in charge said, "He's with us."

Therron opened the door and walked inside. The scent of the Outcasts was overpowering in the crew room. Anger charged his soul, as he headed to the bathroom. There on the counter lay the brush. He picked it up and slid it into his jacket pocket.

Leaving the bathroom, he scoured the crew area for anything out of the ordinary. Once again, he found nothing. The Outcasts were getting good, but he was better.

Another agent entered the room. "Find anything?"

Therron shook his head. "Nothing, I just don't get it though, where could they be?"

"When we know, you'll know." The agent showed him the door. "We're going to secure the room, so get anything you absolutely need."

Therron opened his jacket. "I got my brush, that's all I need." Better to be honest and out in the open, he thought to himself.

The agent nodded and Therron walked out. He stopped to talk to his boss for a few minutes before, getting in his car, and heading to Raven's Hood Manor.

TWENTY EIGHT

Mandy stretched, then reached over to touch her man. She found empty, cold sheets. Sitting up, she looked around the room, certain he must be here or in the shower.

Getting up, she looked in the bathroom and found it empty. "Therron," she called, hoping against hope he'd somehow answer.

Silence met her ears. Pulling on her robe she walked downstairs, certain he was simply having coffee with Frank and Kit. She bounced down the stairs filled with last night's happiness.

Frank's voice reached her and his words cut her to the core. "I saw him leave and drive away about four this morning. Son of a bitch."

"Now don't go jumping to conclusions, maybe he had to work, and Mandy's just fine," Kit scolded.

She walked into the kitchen. "I'm not fine, if Frank's right." Tears filled her eyes as she sat down at the table. "How could he leave without telling me. I mean we..."

Kit walked behind Mandy and rubbed her shoulders. "I'm so sorry, but maybe he had to go to work, and didn't want to disturb you," Kit said, obviously grasping for straws.

"I'm going to kick his sorry ass! You've been hurt enough by selfish jerks!" Frank stomped across the kitchen and poured her a cup of coffee.

"Here's something hot to drink, Mandy." He set it down in front of her.

She looked up. "Thanks Frank." She took a sip then set it down. "I knew I shouldn't have gotten involved with a man young enough to be my son! Face it, why would he want me? I'm just a flabby old lady." She buried her hands in her face and started to sob.

Frank and Kit stood helplessly, unsure what to say or do to help her.

Windy and Hood trotted over to her and each placed their heads on her lap. She reached down slowly, petting her fur babies. "Aw, sweeties, Mommy is so sad."

Hood tapped her hand with is cold nose. She looked down and swore he shook his head no.

Windy tapped her other hand with her nose and shook her head no. Mandy looked down, and this time she knew, the dogs were trying to tell her something.

"I wish I understood dog, but I don't my loves."

Hood and Windy both stared up at her, their eyes never leaving hers.

"Okay this is a little freaky," said Kit.

"U'm, you think that's freaky take a look." Frank pointed.

Kat, Kelsey and Kirby stood still with eyes fixated on Mandy.

"I think they are trying to tell us something." Frank knelt down. "Here Kirby, come here boy."

Kirby's eyes glanced at Frank, but he did not move. He went back to concentrating on Mandy.

Mandy stood up. "What is it?" she said to the dogs. Outside, a raven cawed. All eyes went to the open window where a huge raven sat on the sill.

The Greyhound Gang walked over to the window locking eyes with the raven, then turning back with all eyes on Mandy again.

"I'm in no mood for this!" Mandy headed straight for the raven. "What the hell do you want bird?"

You could have heard a pin drop when the raven said, "For you to know, my son loves you very much. There is trouble afoot. They have come again and taken his friends. Please do not give up on him." She fluffed her feathers then flew away.

The dogs huffed as one, then dispersed onto the various seats in the family room.

The humans stood frozen in place, jaws practically hitting the floor.

"Say what?" Frank rubbed his eyes.

"What the hell is going on?" Kit whispered.

"I don't know, but remember when I told you he introduced his mother and she was a bird? Well, you just met Mommy." Mandy let out a big breath. "I don't know what is going on, but I damn sure am going to find out."

"You aren't going alone." Frank shook his head.

Mandy went to him. "Frank please don't follow me. This isn't of this world, and those she spoke of are deadly, and immune to anything a human can do."

Kit rubbed her back. "We are here to help you Mandy, don't ever forget that."

Mandy nodded then turned to go back upstairs and change.

TWENTY NINE

Therron pulled in to the barn just as his mother landed. He got out of his car and walked over to her, holding Henry's brush out. "Here's my friend Henry's brush, I hope this works."

"Set it down there on my altar, then open the Book of Shadows to page 345. Please fix it so that it stays open."

Therron did as she requested. His phone rang stabbing through the thick silence. Looking down he saw his boss's name. "I've got to take this Mom."

Lady Raven pushed her beak into the hair brush and slowly extracted a single hair. Dragging it across the altar, she dropped it in the cauldron.

"Okay, I'm on the way back. I'll be there in ten minutes." He turned to his mother. "I'm sorry, Mom, but they have a medevac job and no other ships are available. He has another pilot coming in and I'm the only other one who happens to be close enough to take this call. Will you be okay until I get back?"

Lady Raven bobbed her head up and down and fluffed her feathers. "Go, go Son. This spell is only for one. Quick it will be. Quick it will show. Where they are. Where to go."

"I'll be back in no time." He kissed her on the top of her coal black head. "Love you, Mom."

He wasn't gone long when a sleek Mercedes sports car roared down the driveway and skidded to a stop in front of the barn. If a bird could smile, Lady Raven did when Mandy walked in.

"I was hoping you'd come," Lady Raven said.

Mandy stopped dead in her tracks looking first to the bird and then back to her car. Yes, that was definitely her car and a bird was definitely talking. With two of her fingers she pinched herself on the arm hard. "Ouch!"

Lady Raven fluffed her wings and shook her feathered body. "My dear I assure you that you aren't dreaming. This is really happening."

Mandy walked forward to where the bird was perched. "Okay, let's say this is really happening and you are a bird talking to me..."

"I am a raven dear, not a bird." She pecked at the cauldron. "Now I need your help. I am a very powerful witch, but since I have no arms presently, I'm only able to do so much spell work with this beak of mine."

"I'll do anything to help Therron." Mandy walked over to the altar and peered down at the raven. "What do you want me to do?"

"I am, no we are, doing a spell to find Henry Fresco, Therron's pilot friend, who has been kidnapped by the Outcasts."

"Kidnapped? Just who are these Outcasts? Are they the same ones that were attacking me the night I first met Therron?"

"Yes, they are the same. Outcasts are evil vampires, who have broken from the ranks within the Adulane Race. They are responsible for much of the horror and evil the human world experiences. Therron is one of the chosen few, both hunter and healer. His job is to track them down and slay them." Raven peeked at the cauldron.

"Why would they kidnap a pilot? Is he a healer and hunter too?" Mandy asked.

"No, he is a human. I do not know the reason, but I do know that, my Therron is very upset. Henry is a true friend to him."

Mandy looked around, searching for Therron's car.

"He is not here, my dear. He was called in to do a medevac. He is the only one close enough." she said.

Mandy and Lady Raven looked at each other eyes wide.

Mandy held up her hands. "What if they sabotaged the helicopter knowing that Therron would be the one to respond? Then made a call requesting it?"

Lady Raven stretched out her long black wings getting ready to take flight. "This spell will have to wait. I believe you are right. I can sense it now. I have failed my son."

"You did not fail him, yet. We are both powerful and fearless witches. These Outcasts will not win. They will not take Therron!" Pulling out her keys Mandy raced back to the sports car. "You go to the hanger now and I'll get there as soon as I can!"

Lady Raven pumped her wings up and down and took off. "Be careful and be safe, Mandy. The others are evil and will stop at nothing to kill you, me and Therron!"

Mandy watched the raven fade away from view as she stomped on the gas, peeling out down the driveway. She didn't know how, but her GPS suddenly sprung to life telling her the route to take to the hanger.

She dialed Therron's cell phone and it rang and rang until voicemail picked up. Hastily, she left him a message, praying he got it in time.

Fifteen minutes later she charged into the lot coming to a screeching halt in front of the hanger. Panic shot through her! The hanger sat empty.

Three men in dark suits surrounded her car. She opened the door and got out. "Where did the medevac go?"

One of them looked down at her. "Just who are you lady?" He fingered the gun at his side.

"I'm the pilot's girlfriend and a paramedic to boot, buddy, so cut the shit!" Mandy glared at the three men who suddenly backed down.

"U'm, they took a job to some place called Sandyston. What is going on, Miss?"

"We believe the chopper has been sabotaged. There are other...., uh, people that Therron, I mean Jessie, has arrested as a state trooper who want him dead." She lowered her eyes, hoping against hope they bought her feeble last minute story."

"Shit!" The man who'd glared at her did a half turn and ran across the parking lot and into the hanger. There he spoke in hushed tones to another man who appeared to be in charge.

Behind Mandy a raven crowed. She glanced over her shoulder and nodded. The raven took off, heading in the direction of Sandyston. Please God, let her get there in time to warn him.

The man in charge strode purposefully towards Mandy. He held out his hand which Mandy shook. "Hello, I understand you have reason to believe the medevac has been sabotaged?"

She nodded. "Yes sir. I don't have all the facts, but Jessie told me about being threatened. He played it down, but now with the kidnappings and sudden medevac request for an out of service chopper leads me to believe it very well may be sabotaged."

"We've called the dispatch center and they have advised Falcon 1 to come back to base. They have confirmed the call was unfounded. Let's pray this is nothing more than a false alarm." He turned and walked back to the hanger.

Mandy smiled sadly at the men who remained standing by her. "Please let me know as soon as you hear something."

One smiled back at her encouragingly and then saluted. "Will do."

Mandy felt helpless waiting at the hanger, yet wait was all she could do right now. She prayed Lady Raven would get to him in time and help save him and the flight crew on board.

THIRTY

Therron gripped the stick of the blue and white BK117 just as he heard a loud snap. Something was wrong, terribly, terribly wrong. His co-pilot, a man he'd never worked with before, sat paralyzed at his controls.

The chopper began its death spin, round and round. Quickly, Therron cut the engines and then the rotor head which stopped all autorotation. It stopped the ability to forward move, or actually control the aircraft, but it was better than spinning out of control to their deaths.

"Arnie get in the game! I need some help here!" Therron yelled through the headset.

Just then the other pilot turned his head, looking directly at Therron with a huge smile on his face. Unclipping his seatbelt, he opened the door and jumped out, disappearing into thin air.

The medic and nurse in the back held on with all their might as the helicopter began to free fall.

"I see a field off to the left!" yelled the medic.

Therron took control of the situation, manipulating the throttle to yaw the chopper to the left.

The tree tops were coming fast to meet the craft and it meant sure death. Suddenly, as if by magic, the BK117 held its altitude just skimming briskly over the tree tops and moving to towards the open field.

In his mind, he could hear his mother. "I've got the tail between my claws, so keep doing whatever you're doing so you can make it over to the field. I'll keep her level until you're down.

Therron leaned forward and glanced back at the tail. His saw that he had heard her right, his mother gripped the tail with huge talons, her eyes closed, deep concentration on her beautiful feathered face.

You got it, Mom, he sent back. "Your eyes will close and you will sleep, until we are down and safe on the ground," Therron said into the headset.

Behind him the medic and nurse closed their eyes slowly as they peacefully fell into a deep sleep.

Using the power of his father and mother, he levitated the giant chopper. "Falcon 1, use your wings. Sail far and sail fast, over the hills, in a mad dash. Landing safely and not too hard, in the field, in the yard. We will be well, we will all survive, keep it going and we will thrive. Now I command you, to do as I say, with no delay. So mote it be."

The helicopter floated silently in the sky and landed gracefully in the middle of a field deep within a state park known as Stokes State Forest.

Before Therron woke up his sleeping team he jumped from the chopper to check on his mother. She lay crumpled in a ball in the thick foliage. "Mom! Mom, are you okay?"

Weakly, all strength gone, Lady Raven lifted her beautiful feathered head. "I have drained all my energy. I need a safe place to rest so that I can regain my power, Son."

Therron bent down and gathered his mother into his arms. Carrying her to the chopper, he wrapped her in his jacket and set her on the co-pilot's seat. Her chest heaved with each labored breath she took.

He'd never seen her like this before. He couldn't lose his mom now, not after all they'd been through. Using his senses, he found his lady. She was speeding, no shocker there, he though with a smile on his face. Her car was heading this way.

Gathering his mother in his arms, he stood outside the ship, glancing in the windows to make sure the crew still slept. "Take me now straight to her, this I command!"

His spirit left his body and gently cradling his mother, they appeared moments later in the speeding Mercedes sports car.

"Ahhhhhhh!" Mandy yanked the wheel to the left crossing over the double yellow line. A horn blared from a vehicle heading right at them. Therron grabbed the wheel and pulled it back. "Put on the brakes and pull over, Mandy!"

Quickly, she regained control of herself and did what he'd asked. "Oh, my gosh! What the hell? Who are you?" Her mind could not come to grips with his sudden appearance.

"Mandy it really is me. I know this seems unbelievable to you, but I need your help right now." He unrolled his jacket showing her Lady Raven.

"Lady Raven! What happened?"

The huge coal-black bird barely lifted her head.

"She saved us from going down. The Outcasts sabotaged the chopper and one came along as my co-pilot. Without her, we would be dead. I need you to take her and heal her. I have to go back to the ship. My crew is there in a vulnerable sleep state. I swear I will explain it all to you later." He leaned in and kissed her.

Mandy exhaled, kissing him back. "Leave, hurry and don't worry about your mother, of course I will help her."

With that he was gone.

"But wait! Where are you, Therron? How will they find you and your crew?"

No answer came as she found a safe place to turn around. She dialed her phone. "Kit meet me at Serenity Farm and have the altar set up, I need your help. Please summon the coven."

The coven had not been summoned, or in the same place in years. This was going to be a powerful night and she hoped the power came in time to save the Lady.

THIRTY ONE

The Outcast put his foot on the door jam and hoisted himself inside. The flight crew wasn't dead, just asleep. Well he'd take care of that nice and quick. He pulled the dagger from his belt and yanked the females head back to slice her sweet carotid.

His eyes widened in surprise as the stake went into his back and out through his heart. He dropped dead, still in his flight suit.

Therron pulled his body out and dumped it on the ground. He had already thought up a logic explanation for the dead body. He would simply explain how the poor guy panicked, undid his seatbelt and tried to jump. Poor Arnie had impaled himself on a jagged piece of wood.

He activated the locator device then whispered, "Open your eyes, you are safe and well. We crashed landed hard, but we survived. You will feel sore with bumps and bruises, but nothing more. Open your eyes and step out of the door. So mote it is."

The flight crew opened their eyes, looking first at each other and then got out to check on the pilots. Therron sat belted in the right front of the craft. He appeared dazed. The other pilot lay in the woods off to the left.

The flight nurse stayed with Therron while the medic rushed to help the other pilot that they'd just met that day.

"He's dead." The medic walked back over to the nurse and Therron. "Impaled himself on a tree branch. I've only known him for a short time, but I feel horrible."

The nurse wiped a tear away. "Let's have a moment of silence for Arnie."

Therron rolled his eyes before he closed them for 'the moment of silence.' After a couple of seconds, he opened them. That was long enough for the sick bastard who caused this in the first place.

"So how are we going to get out of here?" the nurse asked.

"I've activated the emergency signal. They'll find us in no time, but the hike in is gonna take a bit."

"By the way Jessie, that was some amazing flying. I know your co-pilot froze up and how you got us down in one piece, I'll never know." The medic slapped Therron on the back.

Be glad you'll never know, thought Therron. "Thank you, I'm just happy you two are okay."

The night slowly crept in as they waited for the rescue teams to find them. Silently Therron prayed for his mom. Please God and Goddess, let her be well.

THIRTY TWO

The night was still. The moon full and bright. Not a breeze to feel, or a sound to hear, as the thirteen coven members walked softly into the sacred circle of protection. Precious flat stones formed the circle, each carved with words vital to the Wiccan religion.

Harm None, Blessed Be, Air, Fire, Water, Earth, and Goddess, were just a few of the words glistening with sparklingly jewels in the moon light.

Each witch had dropped what they were doing to come help Lady Raven. Mandy, Kit, Kandy, Lady Rorry Maveen and Connie made up five of the group.

The others were an eclectic group. There was Kerri Ember Starling, a witch of many years. Her long blonde hair flowed freely around her purple gown.

Erinna DeLuna, the current High Priestess of the Santiago Coven, once ruled over by Lady Raven stood quietly at her old friend's side. Erinna's hair, which was long and gray, was drawn back in a ponytail. She wore a silver crystal belt wrapped around the waist of her ankle length maroon gown. "We will heal you my old friend and soon you will rule Santiago again by my side."

Lady Raven nodded her feathered head slowly, too weak from blood loss to do anything else.

The rest of the witches watched the powerful priestess gently speaking to the sick raven.

Chad Trinity, one of the two male witches present, stood a foot taller than anyone else. His hair was light blonde with a touch of gray at the temples. He was an old soul and a very powerful witch.

His counterpart, Alan Crowe, was much younger than Chad and yet he was a very powerful witch in his own right. His black hair glistened beneath the full moon as he pulled on his black cape.

Deborah Reinfire, wearing a bright blue gown, stood next to her friends and fellow witches, Windra Dragonfly, and Janae Starfire. Each was fairly new to the coven, but not new to Wiccan.

Janae's pink gown, contrasted nicely with Windra's teal and gold cape. Nervous, but anxious to help, they clustered together waiting for instructions.

Everyone had smiles on their faces as they watched the last witch arrived. Arleeina Light, was one of a kind. If there ever was a witch who could be called a hippie, it was her. Her tie dyed gown glowed with scattered crystal peace signs.

"Arleeina!" Mandy gave her old friend a hug. "Now we can begin! We need to move fast as

Lady Raven is gravely injured. It will take everything we have to save her."

Kit showed each witch to their place inside the circle of protection.

In the middle of the circle stood the Wiccan's Altar, which was made up of a large boulder with a huge flat, polished Turquoise stone molded to the top. In the center, on a blanket of down, lay Lady Raven.

The seven greyhounds quietly entered the circle. Separating, they each lay down, watching, waiting.

Mandy leaned over the altar, lightly stroking the nearly unconscious Lady Raven. Therron's mother hadn't let on as to how gravely she was wounded until he had left them. Her beautiful wings were nearly severed and talons were bleeding and torn to shreds.

"How are you doing, Lady Raven?"

"I fear I am dying, Mandy. I have been gone so long, who is going to come help me?" She turned her head, beak flat against the down comforter and looked up at Mandy through a black beady eye.

"Lady, when I put out the call for help so many responded that I had to turn some away. There are thirteen witches with the power of the God and Goddess behind us. You will be healed.

Mandy turned to face the group. "Everyone please go to your places. We must hurry, as she is weakening more every moment."

The witches circled the altar as Mandy held out her blue healing crystal wand, pointing it towards the circle's edge. Quickly she invoked the guardian elements of fire, water, air and earth, casting a circle of protection to keep outside entities and evil from harming all within. "Let us begin."

Gently Mandy picked up Lady Raven, holding her carefully while Lady Maveen and Kandy bathed her with Rosemary water.

Connie struck a match and lit incense of Eucalyptus to promote healing, protection and purification. The scent filled the circle.

"Let us all focus our intentions and put energy and purpose into the candles and oils so they are programmed to accomplish their tasks." Mandy stepped forward and stood in front of a deep purple candle.

Picking up a glass container, she opened it and dripped Dragon's Blood Oil onto her palms. Rubbing them together she coated the purple candle from wick to end which would draw powerful energy. Quickly, she picked up her amethyst covered athame and stepped back into the circle of witches surrounding the altar where Lady Raven lay in the center. Lady Raven strained to stay alive, her breathing shallow and slow.

"This one we must do together witches. Please heat your athames in the cauldron fire then step forward and touch the tip. Recite our spell as we planned. Hurry now or it will be too late!" Lady Maveen said.

The thirteen witches each placed the tips of their heated athame and watched the deep purple candle flame to life.

"United we stand, to heal the Lady of this land. Purple flame and Dragon's Blood fill us with strength, boosting our magical powers and our ranks. Intense healing we will impart, quickly now unite our hearts!"

Wind whipped through the trees, as gray clouds floated over the full moon.

Quickly Kit covered her hands in a blend of cassia and rosemary oil before picking up a medium sized white candle. "With this healing oil, I do coat for Lady Raven, to promote vitality, healing, health, protection and success. Go forth now and do your best!" Placing it in the clear holder, she stepped back.

Lady Kerri Ember stepped forward, dipping her amber jeweled athame in the hot cauldron fire. Lifting the athame, she lit the white candle with its heated tip.

"So mote it is," said the coven of thirteen in unison.

A black candle stood next to the purple in an onyx holder. Connie stepped forward and coated her hands with cedar wood oil. Its sweet scent filled the air.

"With this oil, I do coat to purify, banish and repel all negative energies as we spell. Using this,

I command it to absorb all of Raven's injuries and health to be restored."

Stepping forward, High Priestess Erinna De Luna laid her athame right in the fire where it got good and hot. Focusing all her intention on the heated tip, she lit the candle.

"So mote it be," The coven said in unison.

The wind swirled around the altar, dipping over and under the candles, but never putting out their flames. Lady Raven's feathered body shuddered.

"Hurry now!" Arleeina said, as she picked up the orange candle and coated it with peppermint oil from wick to end. "Peppermint oil and candle of orange fill Lady Raven with energy to harness. Use us all in the coven of thirteen, to send to Lady Raven these things unseen - vitality, health and strength, restore her now as the Queen!"

Picking up his athame from the fire, where it lay charging with heat, Chad Trinity quickly lit the orange candle and stepped back into the circle.

"So mote it be!" The thirteen coven members said in unison.

The fire leaped into the air from all the lighted candles. Above them in the darkened sky, huge bolts of lightning shot across the pitch black atmosphere with not a single drop of rain falling.

The wind eased underneath Lady Raven's still form and lifted her into the air, holding her so that she was hovering over the altar and candles.

"We must hurry now or I fear it will be too late! Complete our spell with post haste!" Mandy shouted into the wind!

Stepping forward, Deborah picked up the last remaining candle which was light blue. Beside her, Alan dipped his hand into oil of lavender and coated the candle from the wick, down to the end.

Beside them, Windra and Janae picked up their heat charged athames and lit the blue candle. Its fuse burst with light, filling the altar with a glow. Lady Raven's beak opened and closed faster and faster.

As a group, they began to chant the last and most powerful spell.

"Blue is for healing, peace and rest. Lavender brings tranquility to banish stress. Together our powers unite as one. Goddess and God let this be done. The healing of Lady Raven we command to commence. Do it now and spare no expense!"

The thirteen witches standing in the circle around Raven raised their individually jeweled wands and pointed them to the sky. "So mote it be!" they said in unison.

Above the altar the sky and clouds began to gain speed, swirling faster and faster forming into a vortex directly above the failing raven. From the heavens, a stream of yellow, heat filled, healing light energy flowed down and engulfed Raven.

Arms trembling from the raw energy, the witches struggled to keep their wands alight until the healing was complete. Slowly, the yellow light retracted as the sky became still and the churning wind ceased.

As one, the witches lowered their wands and gazed at the altar. Before them Lady Raven lay still, her breathing even and strong. Both of her wings were now healed and shiny with health, all sign of injuries gone.

Mandy leaned forward. "Lady Raven can you hear me?" She laid her hand gently on the bird's wing and stroked it lightly.

A black eye popped open. "Mandy, is it you?"

"Yes Lady, it is I. The spell is complete. How do you feel?"

The other witches moved closer as Lady Raven slowly held up her head and looked each one in the eye. "I never knew I had so many friends who cared. Thank you is hardly adequate for I am healed." Tears gently dropped from her eyes.

Mandy leaned in and kissed the top of Raven's head. "We love you, Lady Raven. Now you rest. I have a bed all ready for you upstairs."

"No child. I want to be with you all for a bit longer. I haven't felt such loving energy for a very long time, not since I was turned into a raven. Is Therron back yet?"

"Not as yet, Lady Raven, but Frank went to pick him up. The rescue team finally got to them and he should be home any minute," said Kit.

Feeling exhausted, Mandy nodded. "Let's all go inside for something to eat before we do the locator spell to find Therron's crew."

The group of witches, greyhounds and one very sleepy but healthy raven entered Kit's kitchen. They all knew there was much more ahead of them to accomplish this night, but for now, they needed some time to reenergize.

THIRTY THREE

Frank pulled into the Blue Ridge Rescue Squad and saw Therron arguing with the EMT's. He got out and walked over to the group.

"I see your charm is really impressing these folks," Frank said, slapping Therron on the back.

Therron relaxed at the sight of Kit's man and a fellow trooper. "I don't mean to be a pain, but I'm fine, really."

Jan, who was known to be a very experienced EMT, looked back at him in total disgust. "I don't care if you are Superman, you just crashed a helicopter and you need to be checked out by a doc!"

"She's got a good point," Frank said.

Therron turned, glaring at him, his eyes turning a bright red. Frank stepped back and held up his hands.

"Whoa buddy, take it down a notch!" Frank turned to Jan. "I really appreciate what you are saying and I agree with you, but he doesn't and he isn't going to see the doc. If I promise to have him checked out, will you let him sign RMA?"

Jan stood with her hands on her hips. "Fine, but you had better have him seen by a doc and soon!" She put the clipboard with the RMA already on top of it. "Sign here."

Therron looked Jan in her eyes with his now light amber eyes. "I truly do appreciate all you've done, Jan. I promise I will get checked out. Thank you." He signed the paper, releasing the squad from liability.

Jan nodded. "No problem. Take care of yourself." She turned and walked back into the squad building.

Frank stood off to the side leaning against his pickup truck. Therron walked over to him.

"I'm really sorry for getting angry before and glaring at you. I just want to see my mom and Mandy and make sure they are both okay."

Visibly Frank relaxed. "I understand that, but what the hell was that little eye thing you had going on?"

Here it goes. Once again another trooper is going to scorn me, thought Therron.

"I mean, I've seen some pretty weird stuff since meeting and being with Kit, but that—that was..."

"What do you think it was Frank?" Therron stood in front of him. "Go ahead and mock me, just like the other troopers do. I'm very, very different from you Frank, in many ways."

Frank nodded. "First, I can see that. Second, I have no intention of ever mocking you. For the first time in as long as I have known Mandy, she's happy. So whatever or whoever you are, we will work it out. Okay?"

Therron smiled so wide his fangs showed. "Thank you for that. I promise I will always do my best to make Mandy happy."

Together the men got into the truck and drove off to Serenity Farm.

THIRTY FOUR

The Outcasts screamed in rage at their failure to kill Therron in the chopper crash. The remaining three turned towards their captives.

"These humans are very important to Therron. He will come." The leader looked over the terrified flight crew and pointed to pilot Henry Fresco. "You stand up."

Henry stood up on wobbly legs facing the vampire.

"Call your friend Therron and tell him we are going to kill you if he does not do as we say."

"Who the hell are you?"

The leader backhanded Henry across the face. "You don't get to ask questions, human. Do as I say or I will kill you and the next human can call Therron."

The Outcasts laughed and the three of them nodded in unison.

The leader thrust a phone into Henry's hand. "Dial him now!"

"Okay, okay, but who is Therron?"

"I forgot Therron has used a new name this lifetime. Call the one you know as Jessie."

Henry put in number of the man he knew as Jessie and hit send. It rang three times before Jessie answered.

"Jessie, it's Henry. We've been kidnapped by some crazy ass friends of yours. They say if you don't do what they say, they are gonna kill us—and Jessie, I believe them."

The leader grabbed the phone out of Henry's hand and pushed him down onto the floor. "Hello Therron, do you know who this is?"

Cold terror grew inside Therron's chest. "I know who you are, Bragg. If you hurt my friends, I will kill you, and your family!"

Frank inhaled sharply next to Therron. "What's going on," he whispered?

Therron shook his head. "What do you want, Bragg?"

"I want you, Therron and I want you to come alone or your friends are dead."

"If you harm them..."

"Shut up! You do what I want! I am in charge, not you!" Bragg shouted.

Henry and the others shrunk into the corner of the small room as more vampires walked in through the door. By the time the door closed there were twenty more of them.

Huddled next to Henry the flight nurse whispered, "What is going on?"

"I don't know, but it has something to do with Jessie." Henry rubbed his back where it had impacted the floor. "He's our only hope."

"If you show up with anyone else your friends are dead." Bragg hung up. "He will be here within the hour. I can't wait to put the final dagger in his heart."

"What are we going to do with them?" said one of the Outcast, pointing at the hostages.

"They are our assurance he will show. Once he does, and he's dead, they are all ours. We are going to feast tonight!" Bragg fist pumped the air and the other vampires joined him.

THIRTY FIVE

"Look Frank, I can't tell you anymore. You've already heard too much. Drop me off here and go home."

Frank floored the truck. "No way! We're just minutes from home and a whole flock of witches..."

"Coven," interrupted Therron.

"Fine, there's a whole coven of witches there and I'm sure they can help with whatever is going on."

"Sorry to do this Frank, but I must go. Tell Mandy I love her more than anything in this world. Tell my mother I love her and I will see her next lifetime."

"Next what?" Frank slammed on the breaks coming to a halt on the side of the road. The seat next to him was empty. "What the hell?"

Flooring the truck he headed home arriving there five minutes later. He jumped out and raced into the mansion. "Kit!!!"

Kit ran to him. "Frank what is it? Where is Therron?"

He was visibly shaken and white as a ghost. "I don't know what the hell is going on here, and I don't care right now," he said as the rest of the witches and greyhounds joined him in the foyer.

"Therron got a phone call on the way here. Something bad is going down and it has to do with the kidnapped flight crew. One minute he was sitting in the seat next to me and the next minute, it was empty. I mean empty! He was gone!"

The coven inhaled as one.

"He said to tell Mandy he loves her more than anything in the world and to tell the bird..."

"Raven," the group said in unison.

"Sorry, the raven that he will see her in the next lifetime. I mean, what the hell does that mean?"

Kit guided Frank into the kitchen and sat him down in a chair. "There is so much to tell you, my love, but we don't have time. We need to find him now!"

Mandy stood frozen at Frank's words, until Lady Raven flew weakly over and landed on her shoulder. "We must do the locator spell now my dear, before it is too late."

Mandy shook her mind free. "Let's do it!"

The witches ran to the altar as Frank watched them from the kitchen.

Quickly, Mandy called in the guardians and formed a protective circle. The coven of thirteen gathered around the altar interspersed with greyhounds.

"Kerri Ember, will you please lead the spell. I am far too involved to be effective." Mandy stroked Lady Raven's feathers, comforting her.

Kerri Ember nodded, stepping forward. "Your love is strong, Mandy and so I will use you to act as a conduit to Therron. Please come here."

Arleeina took Lady Raven gently off Mandy's shoulder.

Kerri Ember faced Mandy. "I know this will be difficult for you, but I need you to focus on Therron and your love for him. You have been connected through a previous lifetime as well as this one. Draw on that!"

Mandy placed her hands on the altar and closed her eyes. "Therron, Therron, come to me. I need you now. So mote it be!"

The other witches lay their jewel gilded wands upon Mandy.

Kerri Ember was the last to place her wand on Mandy's shoulder. "Together!"

As one the witches begin to spell.

"Therron Reyes-Mythos we command you now show us the way to help you and how. With this spell we locate you quick, lending our powers with a conjuring trick. Relegate the Outcasts to their tombs, with our magical indigo brooms."

Stakes will fly into the Outcasts chests, no matter what their powers, they will not best. Fly we will, by the moons faint light, swooping in to win the fight."

Releasing their wands from Mandy as she lit a white candle coated in carnation oil, they pointed them skyward. Bright streaks of powerful energy, each matching the jeweled colors of their wands, shot upward.

"So mote it be!"

In the scrying mirror on the altar, Therron appeared entering an old industrial area of abandoned buildings. Broken windows reflected his movements in the soft glow of the moon.

"I know exactly where that is! Come on, it's right off of Route 15 in Dover, New Jersey!" Alan Crowe shouted through the winds swirling around the altar. "I release you Guardians and thank you for your protection! Let's fly!"

All the witches, except Connie, grabbed their individual brooms. "Um, no way, I'm not getting on one of those things, besides, I don't even have one."

"No worries Connie, I will guide you, if you will drive. I am far too weak to fly," said Lady Raven. She fluffed out her feathers. "Therron is half witch, so the power will still be strong."

"Okay, come on, Greyhound Gang!" Connie waved her hand forward.

With Lady Raven bobbing up and down on her shoulder, Connie led the way as the greyhounds followed her out.

Each witch readied their brooms, and then they took off in a straight line following Alan. They disappeared from sight as the witch, raven and greyhounds hopped in the dog mobile and followed.

THIRTY SIX

"I am here, cowards!" Therron shouted, as he stood in the middle of the abandoned complex. He focused on the broken windows and doors that were barely hanging on by the hinges each one thrashing and banging about in the swirling wind.

Suddenly, he was surrounded by Outcast—they were everywhere. Holy hell, he thought as he looked around, he was clearly outnumbered!

The flight crew members were on their knees, huddled in a group at the feet of the leader and his two favorite minions. One of them kicked Henry in the side sending him face down onto the jagged pavement.

Bragg stepped forward coming face to face with Therron. "For such a revered hunter and healer, you really are stupid!" He gazed at the Outcast vampires surrounding Therron, their eyes feasting on him. "You haven't got a chance, and neither do your little friends."

The wind whipped around the group of vampires and humans, crashing between them. Therron faced off with Bragg. "You want me, not them. Let them go and you can do what you want."

Bragg spit on Therron. "We are going to do what we want to do anyway, you stupid shit."

With that Therron kicked out and vaulted over Bragg, landing next to Henry. "You okay, buddy?"

Henry's eyes grew wide as saucers as he nodded so slowly, it was barely perceptible.

"Stay down and let me handle this." Therron faced off as the Outcasts reformed their circle surrounding the scared group.

An Outcast flung itself forward, pouncing on Therron, biting and scratching him. Therron pulled a stake from his deep pocket and jammed it into the Outcast's chest. It crumbled into a pile of ash. He kicked it with his boot clad foot.

They were on him before he could react. Biting, tearing, and scratching at his body. Henry stood up and punched one in the face. The flight crew jumped up, each grabbing and pushing an Outcast off Therron.

They were outnumbered and clearly losing. He prayed it would be over quickly and they wouldn't feel pain. His friends from his place of acceptance in this life, fought with everything they had.

Above them the witches formed a circle in flight, faster and faster they flew. The windows in the abandoned buildings began to rattle and shake within their weaken frames.

"Now!" shouted Mandy.

The coven of eleven in the air began to chant. "Glass of death, find your mark, aim it straight at the Outcast's hearts!"

Glass shards shot out from the windows like arrows aimed by archers.

Bragg pulled out a gleaming metal stake and stood over Therron, who was now held prostrate on the ground by the Outcasts. His struggling was useless.

The flight crew lay unconscious and wounded. He'd failed them and there was nothing he could do. "Goddess and Gods please help my friends, shelter them with your comfort until the end."

Bragg smiled, as he raised the stake and stabbed it towards Therron's chest. He died mid thrust, as a shear spike of glass pierced his heart. The stake fell to the ground with a harmless thud as the leader disappeared into a pile of ash.

The vampires holding Therron grabbed their chest, eyes open in shock, as stake shaped shards of glass pierced them. Therron jumped up as they fell into four piles of ash. The remaining Outcasts scattered.

Greyhounds formed an outer circle, nipping and biting any Outcast trying to escape. Winter bit into a fleshy part of a vampire's leg, stopping in shock as it turned to dust in her mouth. She let out a sneeze.

The witches dove from the sky, wands aimed at the vampires. Like lasers, electric shocks flew from the wands, striking the vampires trying to escape.

Motioning with her wand, Erinna aimed a shard of glass at an Outcast running across the dark lot. Kelsey and Kat right on its heels. The shard punctured his back, shooting through his heart and out the other side. Ash fell to the ground as the two greyhounds stopped short, then turned around and went back for more.

Mandy landed next to Therron. Back to back they fought off the Outcasts now numbering less than ten.

Windra aimed her broom at a large vampire charging toward Mandy and Therron. It screamed in pain when she jammed a shard into its chest. She smiled as she watched it fall to a pile of dust.

Suddenly a vampire grabbed the end of her broom, stopping her midair and flinging her to the ground. "Body now absorb this shock, tick tock, tick tock," Windra said. Her body hit the pavement with nary a mark and she was up on her feet and running.

Hood and Kirby charged forward and jumped on top of the Outcast, pushing him to the ground. He jumped up, kicking Hood in the side.

Hood yelped in pain and fell to the ground. Lady Raven fluttered over landing on top of the unconscious dog. Kirby let loose a howl so loud it shook the buildings. Windy, Kelsey, Kat, Winter, and Flash attacked the vampire tearing it to shreds. No spike was needed as their teeth pierced its chest and it disintegrated.

There now only remained one Outcast and it would not be allowed to escape. "This stops now!" Therron shouted as he charged forward with Mandy at his side. He rammed a spike into the last ones chest, smiling with satisfaction as it joined its brethren and became a pile of dust.

Mandy screamed, leaving Therron, she ran to Hood's side and knelt beside him. His body heaved in pain.

"Oh my sweetheart, my little man, please, someone come help me save him!"

The coven now boosted by two, surrounded the clearly dying greyhound. Everyone knelt down and placed their hands upon the white dog with a brown spot over his face. His chest heaved and shuddered with his last breath.

Lady Raven stood on top of the greyhound's shoulder. "Repeat after me coven. Goddess and God we implore, heal this dog forever more. Brave was he, to save a witch, correct his injuries, stitch by stitch. Restore him now, in full health, so he can bow, and receive his due. We love you Hood, rejoin us as you should. So mote it be."

The Coven, tears running down their faces, repeated her words full of grace. Keeping their hands on his body they waited.

Frank knelt beside Kit and added his hand to the mix. Suddenly, Hood inhaled, and could be seen growing stronger with each second. The Greyhound Gang turned their snouts skyward and howled.

Slowly, Hood raised his head looking for his mom.

"I'm here, little man." Mandy leaned down and kissed his white snout. The greyhounds went silent as they each wiggled their way into the circle of witches. Kirby licked Hoods face.

"Huff," Kirby said.

"Wuff," Hood answered weakly.

Lady Raven hopped across his body and onto Mandy's arm, too weak to fly. "He will recover, dear. Let's just get him, along with me, home so we can both begin to recuperate."

Therron and Frank lifted Hood and carefully carried him to the waiting dog mobile. Connie opened the hatch back and they placed the weak, but very much alive greyhound inside.

"Thank you, my wonderful friends. I love you all." Mandy opened the back door and got in slowly, easing her body next to Hoods'. Lady Raven stayed perched on her shoulder as Windy, Kat, Kelsey, Flash, and Winter jumped into the SUV, being careful not to step on Hood.

Connie slipped behind the wheel. We will see you at the farm. She started the SUV and slowly drove away.

Frank looked at the remaining witches and said," I have my pickup if anyone wants a ride back." Holding his girl's hand tightly in his, he smiled at the group.

They all smiled back, before they alighted on their brooms and flew skyward.

"Am I hallucinating? Seriously, what the hell is wrong with me...?"

Kit pinched him hard on the arm.

"Ouch! Why'd you do that?"

She stood on her tip toes and kissed him lightly on the lips. "Still think you're dreaming?"

Frank shook his head, kissing her back good and hard. "My sassy witch, you have some 'splaining to do."

Together they watched the line of witches fly across the moon.

"I'm gonna wake up tomorrow wondering what the hell happened here tonight, but as long as I wake up next to you baby it's all good." He took her hand in his helping her into the passenger side of the pickup. Kirby, who never left Frank's side, jumped into the backseat quietly.

"Let's go home handsome." Kit leaned into the back and pet Kirby's head. "Hood is going to be just fine, Kirby boy. He'll need some, TLC, but he's going to be just fine."

Kirby looked up at Kit, and then Frank, who nodded in agreement.

"Huff," Kirby said. Laying down he fell fast asleep.

THIRTY SEVEN

It was well after one in the morning when Mandy kissed Hood good night, leaving him warm and tucked in a rehab crate in the foster room. "Night, little man, see you in the morning."

Next to him, in another crate, also tucked in warmly, lay Lady Raven. "I love you so much, Mom. I was so worried about you and I am now so relieved you are okay." Therron kissed his mom's feathered black head.

"Good night, my son and his lady." She winked one of her small dark black eyes. "Take your leave now and worry no more. We will both be just fine."

Therron left first and waited for Mandy as she pulled the door behind her, leaving it slightly ajar.

She took his hand in hers and pulled him quietly down the hall to Yellow Cottage. She opened the door and he followed her into the pretty room decorated in various shades of yellow.

She closed the door and locked it behind her. Therron raised his eyebrows and smiled. Without words, he drew her to his solid chest and kissed her.

His lips felt sensual and warm and so right. After all this time and all this sorrow from men, she'd found her true soul mate.

"I love you, Mandy," Therron whispered in her ear, sending chills up and down her spine.

She looked into his eyes, which were now glowing a soft amber. "I love you too, Therron. Promise to never leave me."

"This life time and many to come, I promise you." He wrapped his hands into her long blonde hair and kissed her lips, demanding entrance. She tasted sweet and minty.

Slowly she unbuttoned his shirt and he took it off, throwing it to the floor. Her hands drifted down to his zipper and she pulled it down, her gaze never leaving his.

His hard on strained to get free and sprung out fully engorged as she took him in her hands and slowly moved them up and down.

He thought he'd lose his mind, and his load, if she didn't stop soon. He wanted more tonight than just a quickie. His hand grasp hers stopping her from sliding down his rock hard shaft.

"I want to please you baby and at the rate you are going, it's going to be over before it started."

She removed his hand and smiled. Standing up, she bent forward and with a yank, his pants and boxer briefs lay on the floor. "Therron, I'm in charge tonight, I've got so much power coursing through me right now that I couldn't stop if I wanted to. And I assure you, I don't want to."

His shaft was thick and just the right size. It glistened in the moon light streaming through the open window. She licked her lips, as she knelt down pushing his muscled legs apart. Grasping the base of his hardness she slowly impaled her mouth, sucking and licking with delight.

Therron gasped, his whole body shuddering in a massive orgasm. He wrapped his hands in her hair until it was over. "Holy shit that was the most intense thing I've ever felt." He leaned forward and guided her clothed body on top of his naked one.

He was hard again by the time her lips touched his. Still in her witch's gown, he carefully unzipped the back and shimmied it down her body. She was sky clad underneath, and his breath caught as he realized she'd been so the entire night.

"You are so beautiful," Therron grabbed her bum and grinded her into his rock hard body. "I want you witch, and I want you now."

Mandy straddled him and reached over for the box of condoms in the bedside drawer.

Therron opened a bottle of heated lube he'd kept close to him and put a few drops on his fingers. Slowly he rubbed the outside of her love opening than gently inserted them inside. She felt warm and wet.

Mandy held the condom in her hand as her body moved up and down on his fingers. Her sugar walls slid up and down on his fingers growing wetter and getting ready for him. She locked eyes with his as she slid off and grabbed his hard shaft, sliding the condom on.

She opened for him as his member pushed inside her. Slowly thrusting in and out, never leaving her.

"I love you, Mandy," he said over and over as he thrust deeper and deeper.

"Ohhh!" She grunted and moaned, writhing in pleasure. The tingles started to build and exploded, shattering her into a million sensual pieces. "Therron," she whispered.

A satisfied smile filled his face. "I love you so much, my noisy little witch."

She looked up and smacked him softly. "I am not." Then she laughed. "I hope these walls are sound proof, or Kit and Frank just got a good sound show."

Exhausted they fell asleep holding each other.

THIRTY EIGHT

He woke with a start feeling a pair of beady eyes staring at him. Turning he found his mother sitting on the open window sill. Mandy lay fast asleep at his side.

"Mother, I can't believe you! Can't a guy get some privacy?"

A smile formed on Lady Raven's beak and feathered face. "I'm feeling much better son, thank you for asking."

His mouth popped open in a large 'O' as yesterday came rushing back in full force. "Mom, I'm so sorry." He looked at Mandy. "I kind of ..."

Raven fluffed her feathers and stretched out her fully healed wings. "No worries, my son. I was in love once too. Your Mandy is a good woman. She's a keeper for this lifetime and more. So don't blow it!" She cackled and jabbed her head up and down.

A soft scratch sounded at the door. Mandy woke immediately and jumped out of bed, naked as a jay bird. Therron grabbed a sheet and wrapped it around himself than jumped in front of Mandy, stopping her in her tracks.

"What the heck?" she said as he wrapped the sheet around her and jerked his head towards the window.

Mandy inhaled sharply, her face turning beat red as she saw Lady Raven perched on the sill. "Um... ah..."

"Caw...caw...caw..." Lady Raven flapped her long black wings.

"What is that, your new laugh, Mother?"

Wrapped in the sheets, Therron and Mandy tip toed together towards the bathroom. He turned to glare at his mother just as the door opened and Hood came bounding in, followed by Kit, Frank and the entire clan of greyhounds.

Kit and Frank burst out laughing at the sight of the two love birds wrapped up in the sheets, with the Greyhound Gang doing their best to remove the offending objects.

"Heard there was a party in here!" Frank grabbed Kirby, Kelsey and Kat's collars. "Pretty entertaining!"

"Sorry to intrude. No wait, I'm not really!" Kit bent over grabbing her stomach. Her laughter filled Yellow Cottage. She edged forward, getting hold of Windy's collar, leaving Hood to greet his mom.

Shuffling into the bathroom, Mandy reemerged in a pink robe followed by Therron, in bright green one with huge pink flowers.

Frank burst out laughing. "What I wouldn't give to have a camera now!" He ushered the three dogs out of the room with Kit and Windy close behind. They shut the door with a resounding thud.

"Breakfast in a half hour!" Frank yelled back through the door.

Mandy knelt down and wrapped her arms around Hood. "My little man, how are you feeling? You look great!" She looked up at Lady Raven. "Thank you for saving him last night."

The Lady nodded. "Thank you for saving me, Mandy. I love you both. See you at breakfast!" With a flutter of her wings she was gone.

Hood licked his mom's face and then Therron's hand. He trotted over to the bed and jumped on it. Gripping the comforter with his teeth, he pulled it over himself and lay his head down on Mandy's pillow. "Huff."

"I guess there won't be any morning nookie?" Therron frowned as Hood exhaled and started snoring.

Mandy kissed him. "Care to join me?" She dropped her robe on the floor and walked into the bathroom.

"Now you're talkin'!" Therron dropped the green robe with pink flowers and followed the love of his life into the bathroom. He heard the water running as he shut the door and locked it behind him.

The water felt warm against his legs as he stepped inside. She waited for him wet and ready. His fangs ached to sink into her neck and make her his forever and ever. Never to be parted for lifetimes again.

He shook his head clearing it. That was to be her choice and not his.

Her breasts were moist with droplets of water and her smile nearly undid him. He wrapped his arms around her bare waist and pulled her hard and fast into him. No soul sex this morning, hard and dirty is what he wanted from his sexy witch.

He splayed his hands around her waist and lifted her so that she was pinned against the wall. She spread her legs and slid onto his hard on.

"Wait Mandy, we need to get you protection."

Mandy shook her head. "I fear you not Therron, and I know that as a vamp/witch you have nothing that can pass to me. I want to feel you inside me. I've already made myself ready for you, vampire."

Through hooded eyes, he gazed at this woman he'd loved for hundreds of years. He smile then thrust deep and hard into her slippery love canal. "Ride me baby."

She wrapped her legs around him as he rammed in and out of her. She leaned forward and nipped his ear, then exhaled her warm breath into it.

He went wild with passion, coming with a guttural moan. He spewed his seed into his woman claiming her as his and his alone.

Gently he kissed her, and then lifted her off his cock and they slid down to the floor. His seed washed away with the hot steamy shower.

"Pasta," she said with a breathy laugh.

"Too late, baby." He kissed her, and then licked water off her passion swollen lips. "Damn, I love you."

She kissed him back then slowly stood. Holding out her hands, he grabbed them and she helped him up.

"We are gonna be the talk of the town, and I love it." Taking a loofa sponge, she squeezed soap onto it and then slowly ran it up and down his hairless chest. "I think we'll skip breakfast," she said with a wink.

THIRTY NINE

September 22

"Come on let's get a move on it. The dogs will be arriving in a half hour." Frank knelt down next to Kirby. "You ready to meet the new fosters, buddy?"

Kirby looked up into the eyes of the man who'd saved him from a living hell and licked his face.

"I'd say you are." Frank smiled as his girl Kit, and their other two greyhounds, Kat and Kelsey, walked into the kitchen.

"You fellas ready?" Kit leaned in and kissed Frank.

"Now don't go starting anything, you vixen." He slapped her butt as she walked by.

"Who, little ole me." Kit winked.

Mandy strolled into the room with Hood and Windy on her heels. "Whoa, break it up you two! Some things ain't fit for the kids to see." She laughed, as she covered Hoods eyes with her hands.

"Therron, are you coming with us?" Frank asked.

"He sure is." Mandy stared dreamily into space.

"Yo Sista, snap out of it," Kit said with a wide grin on her face.

"I still can't get used to the fact that the guy is a vampire. I mean, say what?" Frank shook his head. "Witches okay, but a vampire." He shrugged. "What can I say, I like the guy."

Mandy exhaled. "You had me worried there for a minute, Frank. He means everything to me and I want you to get along."

"We get along just fine, as long as he keeps his fangs to himself." Frank grabbed the orange foster collars and leads. "Seriously, he's okay in my book. All we want is for you to be happy."

"I am beyond happy, you guys." Mandy tapped her perfectly manicure hot pink nails on the counter top. "What time do we have to be there?"

"The dogs are arriving around noon and they wanted us there at 11:30. Where is that man of yours?"

The rumbling of a muscle car's engine grew steadily louder. "There he is now." Mandy practically ran to the door whipping it open. Windy and Hood followed.

Therron got out and smiled at the sight of his new family standing on the threshold of Serenity Farm.

"What a great welcoming committee," he said getting out of his Camaro and walking up the steps. He bent down and pet Hood and Windy. Standing up his amber eyes glowed softly as he leaned in and kissed his lady. "Hi baby."

"Hi. I've missed you." She leaned in and softly exhaled her warm breath into his right ear. She felt the shudder of desire go through his body.

"My little witch you are very, very bad and I'm going to have to instruct you on the proper way to greet your man." He lowered his head, nibbling lightly on her neck, but not breaking skin.

She rubbed against him. "Later, hot stuff."

"Okay, break it up before I have to get out the hose and spray you both down with cold water," Frank said, brushing past them.

Therron and Mandy broke out laughing.

Kit eased between them. "What he said."

"Like you two should talk," Mandy said.

Therron and Mandy, hand in hand, walked behind Kit and Frank. The group stopped at the year old maroon BMW SUV, which everyone called the dog mobile.

"Would you two love birds like to go in the Camaro and we'll take the dogs with us?" Frank smiled.

Therron gave him a thumbs up. "Thanks buddy."

"Don't stop off anywhere! We need you both to help bathe dogs. Get me?" Kit stood with her hands on her hips.

Mandy saluted. "We've got you, boss! No problem. I want Therron to really see what happens during an intake so I'll make sure there's no funny business from here to there, promise."

Therron crossed his heart. "Promise."

Kit smiled as she opened the rear door and let the greyhounds in. She fastened their doggie seatbelts on her side and Frank took care of those on the other side.

"I lay odds 5 to 1 he comes home with a foster of his own." Frank nodded his head in Therron's direction.

Therron shook his head. "No way, we already have two dogs and I've never been much of a dog person. They just don't seem to take to me. Know what I mean?"

Frank nodded and pointed his finger. "Sure, I know what you mean. I'll still lay the odds 5 to 1 that you're a goner."

Therron opened Mandy's door and shut it once he saw she was settled. "No way man!"

The two vehicles followed each other and thirty minutes later they pulled into the greyhound intake facility. The facility was a brand new building on ten acres and had been christened the Greyhound Rescue Ranch. The Double Winker's Club had graciously funded the dream Kit had kept alive inside of her for many years. No greyhound was ever turned away, no matter what their history or condition

They parked next to a long silver trailer pulled by a pickup. It had individual dog compartments and carried rescued racing greyhounds up and down the coast dropping them off to various rescue groups.

Kit and Frank got out and put leashes on all the greyhounds before letting them out of the dog mobile. Kirby stuck by Frank's side like glue, looking up at his dad with big trusting brown eyes.

Therron and Mandy walked over to the pack of people and greyhounds. Mandy took hold of Windy and Hoods leashes then wrapped her free arm around Therron's. He looked down and smiled.

Cocking his head to one side he listened. "Are the dogs here? I don't hear a thing?"

"Greyhounds rarely bark and are very well behaved. Plus, they're all scared being in a new place with new people." Mandy lead her man and fur babies up the walk and into the lobby of the rescue.

Once inside the large lobby, they saw it was filled to capacity with volunteers and greyhounds.

Kit, Frank and Mandy released the Greyhound Gang who immediately dispersed. Moving among the scared rescued racers they reassured each dog individually.

Suddenly the hairs on the back of Therron's neck stood up and he got an overwhelming need to look across the room. Something was there, pulling him. He prayed it wasn't another group of Outcasts coming to wreak havoc.

No, it didn't feel malicious; it felt warm, wiggly and happy. "What the heck?" he said out loud.

Mandy frowned. "What is it Therron?"

"Something is over there and it is drawing me, pulling me. I have to check it out. You stay here." He slowly made his way over to the left side of the crowded lobby.

No matter how hard he tried he couldn't get a sense of what it was, nor could he see over the heads of so many volunteers.

Mandy followed him cautiously. If this was trouble, he wasn't going in alone. She headed off to the left, swinging around to cover that side.

Therron eased through the crowd and stopped short at the sight before him. Lying on a blanket of soft pink down, a small three legged brindle locked eyes with his.

The little doe like greyhound was bandaged heavily as if the amputation hadn't been too long ago. Therron knelt by her side. The volunteer handling the little dog looked overwhelmed.

He held out his hand. "Hi, I'm Mandy's boyfriend, Therron. I can take this little lady from here."

Gratefully she shook his hand. "Thank you. She's been crying inconsolably until you appeared. Poor little thing." The volunteer pet the top of the greyhound's head in an effort to sooth her.

"What happened to her leg?" Therron leaned down and ran his hand up and down the little dog's body. Her tail thumped up and down creating a loud noise on the tile.

The volunteer handed him a file. "I haven't had a chance to even read her file she's been so distraught. Now that you're here, she's calmed down so I'll take a look."

Pulling the paperwork out of the manila envelope she scanned it and gasped. "Oh, Sweetheart." Bending down she kissed the three legged brindles head. "She's one of the Shadow Kennel survivors."

"Oh no, poor baby girl," Mandy said as she knelt down by the dog's side. "There were only three dogs that made it out alive. I hope the trainer fries in hell!"

Therron felt a feeling of protectiveness engulf him as he sat down against the wall and let the dog rest her head on his thigh. "What happened at the kennel?"

Mandy looked up from the dog, tears in her eyes. "Greyhound racing is a cruel sport. There are good trainers who truly care for the dogs and do their best to protect them and provide good care. There are also evil entities that take pleasure in torturing the dogs or discard them like trash after they stop winning. The Shadow Kennels were run by a truly evil man named Jamie Good. When he ran into financial troubles he duct taped the dogs' mouths and legs and left them to die of starvation."

The volunteer sniffled. "They were alone there for almost 2 weeks before a trainer from another kennel noticed a foul smell coming from the barn. When he entered the barn he screamed so loud everyone within the compound came running. Despite all their efforts only 3 were able to be saved. 30 greyhounds starved or suffocated to death because of the duct tape."

"This little lady lost her leg because the duct tape cut off the circulation. She was so malnourished they didn't think they could save her, but she's a fighter." Mandy smiled as the brindle licked her hand.

Rage filled up Therron, nearly spilling out in a flood of obscenities. He inhaled deeply three times before he spoke. "What is being done to the trainer Jamie Good?"

"Nothing as yet because they can't find him. He's disappeared off the face of the earth." The volunteer stood up, wiping tears from her eyes. She handed the paperwork to Mandy. "Well, Miss Queen of the Nights, it looks like you are in good hands now." She winked at Therron and walked away to help with another dog.

Therron pet Queenie's back carefully avoiding the bandage on her right shoulder and chest. "So will they have to put her down?"

Mandy shook her head and pulled out her smart phone. "No way. Hold on a minute and I'll pull up a video for you," She held the phone out for him to see. "She's a fighter and will be up and doing this in no time." A video popped up showing a three legged greyhound racing around a field with other dogs. So resilient that the pooch didn't even realize he only had three legs.

"Wow! Look at him go." Therron took the phone and lowered it to in front of Queenie's eyes. "Look at this Miss Queenie. You are going to be good as new!"

The little brindle sneezed then rubbed her nose on Therron's blue jeans. Mandy's eyes bugged out, waiting for him to wig out. Therron only smiled and laughed.

"I can see how dog's don't take to you buddy," Frank said looking down at the vampire and three legger. "So we should probably get her assigned to a foster family, right Mandy?" He winked at her.

"Oh yes, absolutely right. I'll go get the list of foster families and see who works best for her."

Therron looked down at the dog now snoring peacefully. A feeling of love came over him for the little survivor by his side. "About that..."

Mandy and Frank laughed. Kit joined the group. "What were those odds again?"

"Lola, will you please bring over a foster application." Kit waved to a volunteer behind the long counter. She nodded.

"Cool!" Therron relaxed. "So how do we get her home? I mean she can't walk and she'd skin and bones..."

Mandy held up her hand. "My love, you are looking at a group of professional greyhound wranglers. We got ya covered."

Kit knelt down next to Queenie. "You've come a long way little girl." She stroked the dog's long thin side. "Normally a dog with this type of amputation would be up on her own by now, but because of how malnourished she is it's going to be much slower for her."

"I'm going to give Ilaria, from Thera-Paw, a call now and ask her to meet us at the house in a few hours. She can fit Queenie for a new walking harness and guide us through what is to come." Mandy said, then she went outside where it was quiet and pulled her phone out and dialed.

"You okay here by yourself for a bit Therron?" Kit stood up.

"Yeah sure, I guess so."

Kit smiled looking down at the once tough and now mush state trooper. "Hold on, I'll get Frank. He was in your place last year. He'll help you get Queenie to the bathing area and then into the exam room to change the bandage, okay?"

Therron nodded. "Wish my mom was here. She'd know what to do."

Kit shook her head. "Um, since some greyhounds are raised to chase live prey, I'm thinking your mom is better off where she is."

Therron blanched. "Wait, you mean Queenie might eat my mom?" He looked down at the slumbering dog with horror written all over his face.

Kit giggled. "No worries there, Queenie passed her cat and small animal test. She isn't a high prey greyhound which is what you have to be careful of. She'll fit in fine with your mom and the rest of the gang."

"Good, cause I'd hate to have to choose between the two." Therron pet his new fur kid and smiled. "Right girl?"

"Yup, he's got it as bad as I did with you, Kirby boy," Frank said. He knelt down as Kirby sniffed Queenie's butt. Queenie wagged her tail, but didn't open her eyes.

"Oh yeah, she's gonna fit in with the gang just fine." Kit handed Therron the foster application. "Fill these out so we can get you in the system. Then Frank and Kirby will help you guys get to the bathing area, okay?"

Therron, Frank and Kirby nodded.

Connie, with her greyhound Flash at her side, was busy handing out foster applications while Kandy and her little white greyhound, Winter Wonderland, managed the bathing area.

Three hours later, Therron carried a freshly bathed and bandaged Queenie to the dog mobile.

Frank opened the hatch and they gently lay the dog down on her pink down comforter.

"Isn't she just the cutest thing ever?" Therron looked at the group with pride sparkling in his eyes.

Everyone nodded with big smiles covering their faces.

"Frank, you mind driving the Camaro back with Kirby? Kandy is going to take Windy and Hood and meet us at the Farm." Mandy opened the front passenger door.

"Wait a minute. There has never been a dog in the Camaro." Therron crawled in next to Queenie.

"No better time than the present to break her in then." Mandy slowly shut the hatch back and hopped in the front seat. Kelsey and Kat sat quietly looking over the top of the back seat at the new pack member.

"Queenie, I go from being a lonely bachelor to having a family of four to fill my life and dreams. I'm one lucky guy and you are one lucky girl."

Mandy swallowed deeply, filled with such love for her handsome man. She turned to Kit, who was in the driver's seat smiling up a storm. "I'm so blessed."

Kit nodded. "We are both so very blessed, Mandy." Putting the dog mobile in drive she headed for home with the Camaro and Kandy's new GMC pickup following behind.

FORTY

Christmas Eve

Queenie bounded through the falling snow as fast as any of the four leggers. Her joy pieced Therron's heart as he stood shoulder to shoulder with his love, Mandy.

"Just look at her! I can't believe it's the same dog." Mandy grinned.

"Thanks to all of you for helping her through the darkest hours of her treatment." He nuzzled her neck. "I love you, my witch."

"And I you, my sexy vampire." Mandy wrapped her arms around him. "I can't wait to give you your Christmas present later on."

"Christmas isn't until tomorrow." Therron pulled her into his tight body.

She tip toed and kissed his lips, inhaling his scent. "We have a tradition around here, where on the eve of Christmas we each get to give each other one present. I looked long and hard for the perfect one and I believe I found it."

"I have all the presents I need with you, Queenie, my mom and the whole gang. I've never felt more loved or welcomed in my lives, pardon the pun, but it is true. I've always been the outcast." He turned back to watch the Greyhound Gang tearing it up in the snow."

"You will never be an outcast again, my love. Say how are the little babies in the barracks treating you?" Mandy lowered her head with a knowing smile.

"Funny thing about that, they now think I'm the best thing since A positive blood." He tapped his chin with his pointer finger. "You wouldn't know anything about that would you, my powerful witch?"

Mandy shrugged. "Who, little ole me?"

Kandy's GMC pulled up outside.

"Looks like the gang is here." Mandy held the door open for Kandy, Winter, Connie and Flash. "Where's Niki?"

Kandy shook her head. "She hasn't been acting right since the last time we were here. She's moody as hell, I don't even know if she's coming." Kandy leaned in and gave Mandy a kiss. "Merry Christmas Eve."

Mandy kissed her cheek and then leaned down to pet Winter who brushed by her and stood looking out the porch door.

"Gee ya think somebody wants to join the fun outside?" Mandy grinned.

Laughing, Therron opened the door and Winter rushed out, followed closely by Flash. The greyhounds delighted in full out runs, licking the big snowflakes falling.

Connie gave Mandy a hug. "I talked to Niki yesterday. She said she has something very important to tell us. She was very secretive, even though I asked, she wouldn't tell me a thing."

Kandy high fived Therron as she watched Queenie running through the snow. "Awesome job man!"

Connie pushed her way into the line. "Let me see! Wow, look at her go!" She turned and gave Therron a big hug. "She looks wonderful, Therron! I'm so happy for you. So when's the big day?"

Therron and Mandy both looked at her with eyes bugging out of their heads.

"Well, it's only been 4 months ladies." Therron held up his hand.

"Yeah what she said!" Mandy exhaled. "We are really, really happy, but marriage isn't something we even want at this..."

Connie burst out laughing. "You big dopes! I meant when are you adopting her for real?"

Kandy stomped her foot. "Damn, now I gotta take back that blender I got you and everything.... geeze." She slapped Therron on the back.

Mandy smacked Connie in her upper arm. "Dork! You got me."

Therron shrugged. "Actually I have been thinking about..."

Mandy slipped her hand across his mouth. "I haven't exactly had good luck when it came to the old ball and chain. Look how happy Kit and Frank are."

Therron licked her hand, and then nipped at her fingers with his fangs. "We'll play it your way, at least for now, but just to let you know, this man wants a commitment in the future."

Connie shook her head grinning. "Am I in the twilight zone?"

"Yes, yes you are," Mandy said. She kissed Therron boldly. "I am committed to you now and forever my love. You have my heart and you are the first and only man to do so."

Therron kissed her back momentarily forgetting where they were and who they were with. He slammed her against the porch screen, his hands roaming her body.

Connie blushed and turned to Kandy. "Ah, exit stage left!" Quickly they walked into the kitchen and shut the door behind them.

Reality drifted back in, filled with the greyhound's rooing. The couple released their embrace and burst out laughing.

Right outside the door all 8 greyhounds stood shoulder to shoulder rooing and staring at them. Queenie stepped forward. "Huff!" She pawed at the bottom of the screen door, balancing as best as she could on one front leg.

Kirby, who'd taken a real liking to the spunky little brindle walked to her side and let her lean against him. "Woof!"

"Okay you silly kids, everyone inside!" Mandy opened the porch door as Therron simultaneously held open the one to the kitchen.

They each flattened themselves against the wall as the rush of greyhounds pushed through the doors.

"This is the best holiday I've ever had and it hasn't even gotten started yet." Therron held out his hand which Mandy took. "Let's go join the gang."

FORTY ONE

Christmas Eve Day
Raven Hood's Manor

Chanting in unison they circled the lone raven sitting in a bath of Angelica herbs.

White candles sent shimmering light over the dark room. Incense of Rosemary filled the air.

The six witches - Windra Dragonfly, Janae Starfire, Arleeina Light, Deborah Reinfire, Rorry Maveen and Erinna DeLuna glowed with energy.

"For just one night make this right!" said Deborah Reinfire.

"Only once a year let us be clear," said Windra Dragonfly.

"Goddess we ask of you to make her new," said Janae Starfire.

"Young and free she will be. In the form of human born," said Arleeina Light.

"Banish the curse, now we ask, and exorcise her from the past," said Rorry Maveen as she sprinkled black pepper around the altar.

"Daisies are for new born babies, which she will be upon the count of three," Janae said as she laid a bouquet of fresh daisies on the altar.

"One, two, three!" chanted the group.

Lady Raven shifted, feathers dropping off, skin growing in their place. Beak became nose and claws toes.

"Lady Raven in human form let your body now conform, to an age just right for the festivities tonight," said Windra. She lit incense of myrrh which represented the feminine power of the Goddess.

Quickly Janae and Arleeina lifted the baby out of the bath and lay her on the altar cloth.

The baby grew and grew until her feet hung off the altar. She sat up smiling.

"30 is the age that I do choose. I thank you Goddess for this body to use," Lady Raven, now an exotic Latin witch, smiled.

"So now the spell is cast and we know that it will last, until twenty four hours have past. Where upon it will be withdrawn," said Rorry.

"Please grant the lady protection in this form, so that she may transform. Enjoy your family for this night; someday we will make this forever right. Let our love fill you up like an overflowing coffee cup," said Arleeina said.

Eyebrows raised at the last line. Arleeina shrugged. "I thought it was cute."

Smiling, they all said, "So mote it be!"

Naked Lady Raven shimmied off the altar and stood on two human legs for the first time in hundreds of years. Arleeina quickly wrapped her in a warm blanket.

"Now to get you dressed for tonight's festivities!" Rorry pointed to an array of beautiful winter dresses she'd brought from the Goddess Crone.

Lady Raven gazed over the gowns. "Rorry they are all so beautiful! I hardly know which one to choose." She ran her hands over the beautiful fabrics.

Windra picked up a purple gown that had a wide silver and diamond encrusted belt. "This one would look gorgeous on you, Raven"

Raven broke out into a huge grin. "That's the one!" She dropped her robe unabashed at being naked. It felt so good to be a human again she didn't care who saw what.

Windra and Erinna helped her step into the gown and pull it up over her shoulders. They stepped back to admire her.

"Gorgeous!" Janae clapped.

"You are truly beautiful Raven," said Deborah.

Rorry motioned for Raven to come back to the table. She held up a beautiful purple panty and bra set. "I think you'll feel even more beautiful if you wear these." She winked.

"Yes it has been so long I forgot about underwear." Lady Raven giggled.

A knock sounded at the back door.

"Better late than never," said Arleeina with a wink. She opened the door letting Kerri Ember Starling in. She rushed through the door.

She stopped short seeing Raven for the first time in her human form. "Lady Raven you are magnificent! I am so sorry I missed the spell and so happy it worked!" She hugged Raven. "But I didn't come empty handed."

She place light purple tights and silver boots in Lady Raven's hands. "How did you know?" Lady Raven gasped.

"Oh I just know. Now go put everything on and then I'll do your make up. Be quick, you only have tonight and we want you to spend as much time as possible with your family." Kerri Ember shooed her into the bedroom.

"My family," said Lady Raven filled with happiness.

An hour later the witches piled into Kerri Embers big old Cadillac and headed off to Serenity Farm.

FORTY TWO

It was late and beginning to get dark. Therron paced the floor. "Where could she be? I've called and no one is at Raven's Hood. I'm really worried you guys."

Mandy motioned for Kit to follow her over to the small altar room on the main level. She pulled out her scrying mirror. "Let's see what we can see. I need you here for moral support in case it isn't good. Oh please Goddess, let it be good!"

Kit nodded. "I'm here for you." She lit 3 white candles calling in the guardians of air, fire water and earth for protection.

Mandy opened the small fridge and pulled out a purified bottle of water. She poured it into a black crystal bowl. Next she dropped in a Topaz gem to symbolize December. From the drawer she pulled out one of Raven's feathers she'd kept to help during the healing process. She dropped the feather into the water.

Kit and Mandy centered themselves and gazed into the bowl.

"Are you seeing what I'm seeing?" Mandy asked excitedly.

"If you are seeing a beautiful woman dressed in purple than I am."

"How can we be seeing a woman when she's a raven?" Mandy concentrated on the feather.

"Oh, my gosh! She's in Kerri Ember's Cadillac with some of the coven."

"And she's on her way here! Oh Mandy! Therron is going to be so happy!!"

Mandy hugged her best friend. "Let's go out and wait. They are almost here!"

The women walked out and nearly got knocked down by a worried Therron. "Mandy! Thank God, I thought you were missing too. The Outcasts must have my mother. We have to find her!"

Mandy reached up and kissed her man. "She is well, Therron. More well than you can imagine. Kit and I just scryed and saw her. She is coming here now."

"Scryed? What the heck is scryed?" Therron shook his head, running his fingers through his dark hair.

"You mean you've never scryed as a witch before?" Kit said with surprise.

Shaking her head, Mandy laughed. "Oh great hunter and healer scrying is something we witches do to get a vision of what we seek. Tonight we sought Lady Raven."

"Oh boy, did we see." Kit smiled then patted him on his arm and walked out into the kitchen. "And that concludes your first lesson."

Therron looked down into her eyes. "I trust you with my life Mandy. If you say it is so, than I believe you."

She ran her arm through the crock of his elbow. "She will be here very soon."

Together they rejoined the group gathered in the kitchen and family room. All the greyhounds, except Queenie, were decked out in their jammies dancing around the room with everyone.

Therron knelt down and held out his arms. "Come here little girl."

Nearly completely healed, Queenie hopped over to Therron and leaned into his body. She'd amazed everyone with her spunky spirit and will to live. "You need jammies now that your leg is all better."

Mandy left the kitchen and walked into the huge living room where all the presents lay. She picked up a packaged wrapped in pink wrapping paper covered in candy canes.

Therron kissed Queenie's soft snout. "My sweet little baby girl." He heart melted every time he saw the petite brindle greyhound.

Mandy knelt down next to them and handed Therron the present. "I just saw Santa and he wants Queenie to have her present early."

A huge grin broke out on Therron's face and Queenie hopped up and down wagging her long tail.

Therron opened the card on top. "Oh, how wonderful, it's from Kerry McMillian who owns No Nude Hounds. It says: May your little girl sleep tight in her pink jammies tonight.

Congratulations on welcoming your new family member Happy Holidays, Kerri.

He ripped open the package and there were two jammies made especially for his three legged girl. One was soft pink with white sheep and red stars. The other was pink with multi colored teddy bears.

Therron looked at Mandy with tears in his eyes. "I don't think I could be any happier in any lifetime than I am here with you, Queenie and my new family."

She rubbed his back. "I feel the same, my love. So blessed are we to wake up each day actually living the life of our dreams."

He held out the teddy bear jammies. "I have no idea how to put this on her. Can you help?"

Mandy nodded and stood up, taking the jammies from Therron. "It's jammy time, little girl."

Queenie stood still leaning against Therron on her stump side. Mandy slipped the jammy over her head and down her back. She picked up the hind legs to put them in the jammies first. "Just wrap your arms around her for balance so I can get it over her front leg."

A short time later Queenie proudly strutted over to the Greyhound Gang who welcomed her with sniffs and licks.

The doorbell chimed and the tune jingle bells filled the air. "Now who could that be?" Mandy said with a smile.

"Not my mom. She can't ring door bells with her beak." He paused. "Well, I guess she could if she hovered long enough." He stood up and walked into the foyer.

Kit motioned for everyone to follow Mandy and Therron. She held up her finger, covering her lips to tell them all to be very quiet.

Therron opened the door. "Yes can I...." He froze. "Mom?"

There surrounded by her friends and fellow witches stood his beautiful mother in human form. Raven stepped forward and hugged her son for the first time in hundreds of years. "My son, it is truly I."

"You are cured! I have my human mom back! Mandy!" He turned to find everyone standing with mouths open wide. The applause started slowly then built to a crescendo.

Mandy put her arms around Raven's waist and guided her into the foyer. She motioned for the others to follow and join the party.

Lady Raven, now inside the warm and inviting mansion, opened her arms to her son. "Come here and let me hug you, for I only have tonight and then I am back to ole bird beak." She laughed gaily.

Therron turned to the other witches. "You all gave this gift to me?"

They nodded with smiles filling their faces.

"The Goddess in her grace will allow your mother one day and one night a year to be in her human form. She chose tonight to spend it here with her new family," said Rorry.

"Thank you all, I don't know how you did it, but thank you." Therron hugged his mom, crushing her to his chest.

She laughed and pushed away with her hands. "Easy on the goods son, this beauty has to last till morning light."

Therron laughed. "Oh Mother, your beauty hasn't dimmed at all. You are the most beautiful raven in all the land."

She playfully smacked his arm. "My raven form has come in handy through the years, I will admit, but this is the form for which I truly wish."

He wrapped his arm around her waist, as Mandy did the same on the other side.

"I know, Mom. I'm sorry."

"No matter what form you're in, we love you," said Mandy.

Breaking the glum moment Kit waved her hand. "Come on, let's get this party started!"

Two leggers, four leggers and one very special three legger made their way into the kitchen for the Christmas Eve feast.

The doorbell chimed Jingle Bells again.

The Double Winker's Club members looked at each other.

"Has Niki decided to join us after all?" Kit headed back to the door and opened it. Niki stood on the steps with a pretty short haired blonde.

"Hi Kit, sorry I'm late. This is..."

"Lady Willow Morgan," said Kit.

Willow smiled. "I had no idea we were coming to your house Kit. It is so good to see you."

"Come in out of the snow you two." Kit motioned for them to enter.

"U'm, you guys know each other?" Niki stood outside staring in at the two women.

"Yes, for years now, right Kit?"

"I'd say about two or three years." Kit looked from Niki to Willow. "Is this what you wanted to tell us?"

Niki slowly walked into the foyer with her head down. Willow walked over to her and lifted her chin.

"Never be afraid to speak your truth," she stood next to Niki, who now looked Kit in the eye.

"Can I talk with you and the rest of the DWC before the presents? If you don't want me to stay I'll understand and I don't want to ruin Christmas Eve for anyone and..."

Kit held up her hands. "Something has been going on with you for a while now Niki. We've all noticed. You've said some things that really hurt, but you are part of us. We're a family. Anything you have to say won't make us turn against you." Kit pointed to the altar room. "Would you like to talk with us in private?"

Niki nodded. "We'll be waiting in there, okay?"

"Yes, that's okay. I'll go get the others." Kit turned and walked into the kitchen. "I have to steal the ladies of the DWC for a few minutes." She motioned for the members to follow her.

Connie, Kandy and Mandy followed Kit into the altar room. It was small, but big enough to easily accommodate them all.

Kit motioned for them all to sit down in a circle on the plush carpet. White candles flickered in sconces on the wall providing just enough light for them to see each other.

Mandy smiled in surprise at seeing Willow. "Hi Willow what are you doing here?"

Willow smiled back easily. "I believe you are about to find out." She took Niki's hand in hers.

"Go ahead Niki," said Kit.

Niki hesitated, swallowing deeply.

"There is no judgment here Niki. We are your family no matter what." Mandy squeezed her other hand.

Niki exhaled loudly, stress pouring off her aura. "I know I've been acting like a jerk for quite a while now."

Kandy shook her head. "That's for sure," she said sarcastically.

Connie held up her hand. "Kandy, there is no need to be mean. Give her a chance to speak."

Kandy ran her fingers through her short spiked hair. "Sorry, you're right. I've just been so hurt, it's hard not to lash out. Go on Niki."

"I don't blame you for being mad at me, Kandy. I've been going through so much I didn't understand and because I was so confused and trying to deny how I was feeling, I took it out on my family. I am so sorry." Niki reached across the circle and grasped Kandy's hand.

Kandy squeezed back. "I miss my friend."

Niki nodded. "I know, and I miss you too. I hope after I tell you what I have to say, you'll still want me to be your friend."

Willow squeezed her hand. "Go ahead Niki, you need to get this off your chest."

Niki looked each of her friends in their eyes before continuing. "I haven't felt right for a very long time. This is so hard." She paused, looking to her friends and Willow for more reassurance.

"Go on honey, tell us what's going on," said Connie.

"Willow and I are more than friends. I love her." Niki waited for the group's reaction.

Kit held up her hands. "And?"

Mandy nodded. "Speak your truth, Niki."

"I'm gay. I've never felt attracted to men, but I went along with the program figuring there was something wrong with me. Until I met Willow last year."

Willow smiled. "I haven't been the same myself since that day. You kept denying it and pushing me away. You even called me demonic for my Wiccan beliefs."

"Said the same thing to us," Kandy pointed at Connie.

"You really pissed us off that night, but now I get it. You were trying to deny your true self by pushing us all away."

Niki wiped a tear away. "I'm so sorry. I just couldn't believe after all these years that I wasn't straight. That I loved or love a woman."

"Niki we love you no matter what your sexual orientation is," Kit said softly.

"Especially now that you've fallen in love with a fellow witch," Mandy ribbed her.

"So, have you changed your mind about us demonic witches?" asked Connie.

Niki laughed, nodding her head. "I can't believe this, but yes, I've changed my mind. Now, I'm not ready to jump into all the Wiccan stuff, but I know there is something real. I can't deny it anymore, not after falling in love with a witch." She leaned over and kissed Willow.

Kit held up and imaginary champagne glass and the others followed. "To the DWC now and forever!"

"Here, here!" the members said in unison.

"We welcome you Willow to our group," said Mandy.

"Thank you all. I've never felt so accepted in my life," Willow said softly.

"Now let's go open some presents!" Kandy stood up and walked over to Niki. "I'm proud of you. Can we go back to being partners and friends now?"

Niki bear hugged her fellow Wayne cop. "Oh, hell yeah!"

Kandy tussled Niki's long curly black hair. "Let's go brat."

Smiling and laughing the women walked out into the kitchen.

Silence fell over the party goers. "Everything okay honey?" Frank asked.

She nodded. "I'd like you to all meet Niki's significant other, Willow Morgan."

Frank's eyebrows rose. "Well this is a new twist. Nice to meet you Willow, I sure hope you can tame this wild child."

"The wilder the better," Willow said winking.

"TMI!" yelled Kandy, covering her ears.

Everyone laughed.

Frank, the ever gracious host, passed out real champagne glasses filled with Asti Spumante. "To love!"

"To love," said the group of witches, humans and vampire.

"Can we go open our presents now?" said Therron, with the glee of a little kid at Christmas.

Lady Raven took hold of his hand. "I love seeing this side of you, my son."

"Mom, being with you, my love Mandy and my new family is the best Christmas present I could ever wish for."

The group walked into the beautifully decorated living room. A twelve foot, live tree, decorated with white lights and multi-colored Christmas ornaments stood gracefully in the corner. Soft Christmas carols played through the overhead speakers. Stacks of presents lay around the tree, with the special Christmas Eve presents out front.

"This is just beautiful Kit and Frank. Thank you for inviting us into your home," said Lady Raven.

The clock chimed eleven in the evening when the last present was opened. Sated and satisfied, Therron leaned back against the couch next to his mom.

Suddenly he realized Mandy was nowhere to be seen. He started to stand up.

"My son, would you please get me a cup of tea. I'm feeling a bit cold and tired."

"Sure Mom, I'll do that right now." He walked out of the living room towards the kitchen.

Lady Raven motioned for Kit to follow him. "She needs more time!"

Kit followed Therron. "Let me help you get your mother her tea."

"Do you know where Mandy is?" Therron scoped out the kitchen and family room looking for her. Queenie hopped along by his side.

"I'm sure she's around here somewhere. Why don't we get your mother's tea and then you can go look for her."

"Would you mind getting her the tea? I really want my lady. I've had such a great night and I want to tell her so."

Kit stammered, jutting her face forward, motioning for Queenie to help distract him.

Suddenly Queenie started to roo. The other greyhounds came running and surrounded Therron. Stuck in a greyhound traffic jam, he had no choice, but to wait until their song was over. He smiled, momentarily forgetting his quest for Mandy.

Kit walked over to the intercom and pushed the button to Yellow Cottage. The call beep sounded. Mandy opened the connection. "Hello, Therron?"

"No, it's me. The greyhounds are distracting him as you can probably hear, but he's determined to find you. You only have a few more minutes to get ready. Hurry!" Kit whispered into the mic.

"Roger that," said Mandy. She clicked off.

Kit watched Therron playing with the greyhounds as they rooed their song. After ten minutes, she gave the signal. The Greyhound Gang stopped rooing and walked away.

Therron stood alone in the kitchen. "Well that was interesting." His smile was big and his mood light as he headed up the stairs to Yellow Cottage.

Kit, Connie, Kandy, Niki and Willow watched him go.

"He's in for the treat of his life!" Kit said.

"Hope he can handle her! She's been planning this surprise for weeks," said Connie.

"I helped her pick out ... well you know. I'd love to see his face," said Kandy.

Niki and Willow glanced at each other. "We have no idea what's going on, but it sounds fun," said Niki.

Lady Raven came into the group. "Do you know where my son is?"

They all turned to her and smiled, then giggles broke out.

"I don't think you want to see him right now, if you get my drift," said Kandy.

Raven's eyes went big as black saucers. She smiled. "I do know what you mean child and I am thrilled for him. I think Mandy is wonderful and I'll not bother him until the morning."

"Will you still be like this in the morning?" asked Kit.

"Yes child. I have a full 24 hours so I'll be able to have breakfast with my son and the rest of this wonderful tribe."

"Tribe, I like that. Family sure doesn't have to mean blood relative," said Connie.

They all nodded. "How about we get some dessert," Kit said, pointing to the dessert tables. Silently she looked up at the ceiling and mouthed: "Thank you Goddess for this beautiful and loving night."

FORTY THREE

Standing outside the door, he heard soft and sensual music playing. He knocked on the door. "It's me, love."

The door swung open revealing Mandy. The room sparkled with candle light. He inhaled sharply as he caught a glance of what awaited him.

Mandy's breasts looked like two deliciously decorated vanilla cup cakes with cherries in the middle. She wore an edible chocolate G-string with just a tuff of whip cream in her navel. She walked away wearing thigh high black patent pleather six inch heeled boots. Smiling she sat down on the bed, legs apart and wiggled her pointer finger in a 'come hither' motion.

"Mandy, my naughty witch." He entered and shut the door, turning the lock behind him. Slowly, as if he was performing in a strip show, he pulled off his shirt, locking eyes with her. He pushed down his jeans revealing black boxer briefs. His shaft filled with red hot blood, standing at attention and ready to sink into his woman. He walked towards the bed.

His eyes gleamed bright amber as he looked down at the mouth watering sight sitting seductively on the bed.

Mandy smiled, and then ran her tongue across her cherry tinted lips. Her body felt cool and hot all at the same time. She jutted out vanilla cupcakes and ran one finger underneath the right one. Slowly she inserted the finger in her mouth, licking off the icing. She gazed up at him through hooded eyes. "Like what you see, vampire?"

Therron's choked, as she ran her finger between her pert breasts. Two de-stemmed cherries sat on top of the mounds of icing. "In the mood for some cupcakes? I happen to have two, specially made for you."

He knelt down between her open legs and for the first time in a long time felt unsure of himself. Normally he was the one in control, but not with his witch. She was truly his match.

She reached up and gently ran her hands through his hair then pulled his mouth onto her iced jug. He licked it taking in her scent mixed with icing. Gently, he picked up the cherry with his tongue and slid it in his mouth.

Swallowing, he locked eyes with Mandy. "Do you have any idea what you are unleashing witch?"

Mandy did not look away. "I want you, Therron and all that goes with you. I'm no saint baby and I intend to sin my butt off tonight."

"Safe word?" Therron lowered his head and licked her nipple.

"If you feel you need one." Mandy pushed her fun bag into his open mouth, her body writhing with need.

Therron lapped her breasts, freeing them of the icing. "I don't need a safe word, but if you want me to stop, say no and I will."

Mandy nodded looking through hooded eye lids.

"You haven't been the only one planning tonight my love." He reached down under the right post of the foster poster bed and pulled up a chain with a cloth tie on the end. "Are you sure Mandy? Because once I start, I can't stop, not with someone I love and want as much as you."

In answer, she pushed her hand through the cloth tie and stopped once it was around her wrist. With her other hand she slowly slid it down his belly and underneath his boxer briefs.

His love machine felt thick, hot and ready as she began to stroke it up and down. "I think we're both ready now, Therron."

Raising his head his fangs came out. He licked his lips as he removed her hand from his shaft and secured it with the other cloth tie.

Mandy sat on the bed with her hands tied to the bed posts. Her blue eyes never leaving his amber ones as he walked over to the closet and opened it. He pulled out a long spring with a metal hook on the end.

In the far corner of her bedroom he stood on a chair and secured the chain to a round metal plate. Mandy smiled, wondering when he'd had the time to sneak in here and set this up.

Once the chain was secured he reached back into the closet and came out with a black fetish swing. He walked back over to Mandy and untied her from the bed posts.

"My hot sexy witch, you are going to enjoy this. Step through the two larger supports and then step into the stirrups."

Mandy did as she was told and soon was secured in the swing. He picked her up, carrying her over to the hook and attached the swing to it. Gently he released her body to hang in the air. Her back and rear were nicely supported by two wide strips of black material and her feet fit nicely in the free floating stirrups.

He flipped her onto her back and spread her legs. Kneeling between her legs, he pulled the straps and her sex triangle was at his lips.

Mandy gasped as his teeth started devouring the chocolate panties. Naked and glistening with love juice, he lapped it up with his tongue.

Standing, he moved to her breasts and leaned down grabbing and kneading the right one as he sucked and licked it clean of any remaining icing. Switching he licked and squeezed her left one, pinching her erect nipple between his teeth.

Little squeaks of pleasure escaped Mandy.

Immediately Therron stopped. "Am I hurting you? Are you okay, Love?"

Mandy leaned back against the straps and grabbed his head pulling his lips to hers. "I'm more than all right. Do what you want to me, I'll happily take it."

He inhaled deeply. From the bedside table he pulled out flavored warming lube and a purple blindfold. Standing between her legs he squeezed little drops on her love button and opening. Then he slipped the blindfold over her blue eyes.

Grabbing the sling, he pulled her forward letting his hard on slide up and down over her sex. Rubbing, teasing, he brought her close to ecstasy then stopped.

"Therron?" Mandy wiggled in the sex swing.

Smiling, he leaned over and pulled out a tray of ice cubes from the mini refrigerator. Taking one he slowly touched her chest.

She jumped from the cold pleasure. He slid the ice down her belly and onto her red hot triangle. A cold numbing filled her sex center. "You'll last a little longer now baby, I need to fill you up until you explode."

He grasped the swing and swung her around until her opening hovered in front of him. With one pull of the roping he impaled her. Like a wild stallion he thrust in and out of her.

He flipped her over taking her from the rear. She felt hot, wet and ready for action. Her muscled contracted around his shaft as she came with a loud scream. Thrusting, his orgasm built until he shot his seed into her. Quickly he pulled out. Pulling the swing to him he wrapped her legs around him and bent down to kiss her passion swelled lips. "Are you okay?"

A satisfied moan escaped her lips. "Holy smokes, that was intense. I think I'm going to like being submissive from time to time."

Therron's eyebrows rose. "From time to time, my lady and what about the other times?" His cock grew hard looking at her floating there, naked and splayed open for his eyes only.

"The other times, you will agree to let me be a dominatrix. It was once my specialty, although sadly, I have not practiced for many, many years."

Therron pulled off the blindfold and gently held her as he released her body from the sling. Her legs trembled as he held her to his naked body, helping her stand.

She walked to the bed and lay down. "Come to bed, my love and let's rest, so we can play again in the morning." He crawled into bed beside her, warm, happy and satisfied. Spooning, they fell asleep within seconds.

FORTY FOUR

The kitchen was alive with people eating when Therron and Mandy made their way downstairs.

Everyone present turned with smiles covering their faces as the two lovers walked in holding hands.

"Looks like you two had a good night," said Frank.

"She's practically glowing," Kit said to the group as she looked Mandy up and down. "Yup, glowing, I tell ya."

"I don't know whether to hit you from embarrassment, or give you the satisfied smile of total bliss that I am feeling." Mandy turned, then froze as she caught sight of Lady Raven who was still in her human form.

"Oh, my gosh, I think I am going to die. I am so sorry Lady Raven, I had no idea you were here."

Therron gripped Mandy's arm for dear life. "Please, tell me my mother didn't just hear that."

"Nope, can't do that," said Kandy with a laugh.

"That would be a lie, and my mother always taught me to tell the truth," said Connie.

"Just like George Washington..." Frank jumped back as Mandy swatted at him. "Yo Sista, hands off the merchandise."

The group of friends started laughing, with Lady Raven joining right in.

"Mandy dear, I was once young and in love too. Hell, I wish I had a hot man right now to use this beautiful body on."

Henry Fresco cleared his throat. "I'm ready, willing and able my lady." He held out his hand.

Lady Raven inhaled sharply. She looked at Therron who smiled and shrugged.

"I trust him with my life, Mom and if you want to enjoy yourself before..."

Niki and Willow stood with arms wrapped around each other.

"Lady Raven, you've been through so much. Once a year you get twenty-four hours in human form—I say, go for it," suggested Willow.

Lady Raven nodded. "I fear I will hurt you Henry. You are a good man and I am only here for a few more hours in this form."

Henry lifted her hand to his lips and kissed it. "Raven, I have enjoyed this night talking with you and getting to know you. I feel a connection to you that I've never felt with anyone else."

"True Mom, the guy rarely dates."

Henry glared at Therron. "Way to make me look like a stud."

"What I mean is he is very picky and I can't believe I'm saying this about my mother, but he's picked you. Now are you going to waste the few hours you have left or go for it?"

Raven grasped Henry's hand. "I'm about five hundred years out of practice."

"Me too," Henry said with a wink.

Kit discreetly waved for them to follow her upstairs. She opened a room decorated for lovers. "Welcome to Lovers Lair, all you will need to enjoy yourselves is in the closet."

With that she was gone. The two lovers to be entered the room as nervous as teenagers.

"Okay," Frank said. He started cleaning up the table and putting the dishes in the dishwasher.

Kit wrapped her arms around his waist. "I love you."

He turned and hugged her. "I love you too, baby, more than you will ever know. This sure is an interesting tribe we are creating."

Kit nodded. "It certainly is."

Mandy and Therron walked into the family room and were quickly surrounded by a group of happy greyhounds.

Therron knelt down next to Queenie. "How is my little girl doing? Are you having a good Christmas? We're going to open our presents soon."

Queenie hopped at his feet, her three legged jammies keeping her warm and secure.

Windy and Hood nosed Mandy's hand. "How are my two favorite hounds? Did you miss me? I missed you."

From the living room Frank yelled, "Presents are now being opened! Come join us!"

The happy tribe of human, witches, vampire and hound, unwrapped their presents with glee. An hour later the room was filled to capacity with presents, wrapping paper and dog toys.

Mandy and Therron sat together on the couch surveying the Christmas scene.

"I have never felt so welcomed, blessed or loved." Therron kissed Mandy's cheek. "Thank you for being the speed demon you are! Heck, if you drove like a little old lady I'd never have found you."

Mandy swatted him playfully. "Are you calling me old?"

"Old enough to know better than to keep me waiting for one more taste of you." Therron stood up and held out his hand. "I feel the need for a nap my love."

Mandy winked. "Oh, I don't think you'll be sleeping too much."

Frank looked over at his lady and stretched. "I believe I'm feeling a nap coming on too." He held out his hand which Kit took.

Connie and Kandy stood together in the room, surrounded by the carnage of Christmas past.

"Well, I guess it's just you and me kid," Connie patted Kandy on the arm.

"Can you believe that everyone is getting nooky, but us? Santa sure didn't bring me what I wanted this year."

"Let's clean up and get out of here, it's too depressing." Connie bent down and gathered up wrapping paper, then shoved it into a garbage bag.

Kandy wiped away a tear. "I know I should be so happy for everyone, but I feel sad and alone instead. Stupid Mark! Using me like I was just another port in the storm."

Connie dropped what she was doing and hugged her friend. "I know honey, and I'm so sorry. I wish I could make it better."

FORTY FIVE

Back at the Hollowed Hall in Raven's Hood, seven old school witches smiled as they gazed into the scrying ball.

"I believe we have one more spell to do ladies." Erinna picked up her wand glistening with diamonds.

"Yes, we do, and let's make it for two." Windra held out her wand encrusted with jeweled dragonflies.

Kerri Ember stoked the fire, throwing on another log. "Let's bring happiness to the remaining members of the Double Winker's Club."

Janae twirled around the room, her long pink dress floating out. "I love, love."

Deborah smiled. "I'm game, if you are witches."

"I'm so excited for them!" Arleeina flew around the room - literally - lighting white candles.

The witches gathered around the altar.

Erinna studied the altar. "We have all the essentials we need. Let us begin." Before starting the spell, she held out her crystal wand and pointed it towards the edge of the circle.

"I invoke the guardian elements of fire, water, air, and earth and ask for protection." Moving her wand around the room, she cast a

Circle of Protection to keep outside entities and evil out.

Rorry rang a small bell. "On this day of peace on earth, we ask you Goddess for some mirth."

"Kandy and Connie hearts are so alone with nothing to atone and so much unknown," said Windra

With her athame, Erinna lit incense of patchouli. "Patchouli to bring out lust, this we know is a must."

Kerri Ember coated two whites candle from wick to end with ylang ylang oil. "True love & sex comes to them from the use of ylang ylang."

Deborah stepped forward and lit two white candles each of which had a ruby heart shaped stone imbedded in it and the carved names of Connie on one and Kandy on the other. "Goddess, we ask of you to send true love to Kandy and Connie too."

"When that will be, we can only guess. Let this spell do the rest," said Janae.

Arleeina threw rose petals in the air. They softly fell surrounding the burning candles. "Roses are the color of red, petals so light and bright, they light the path for men so right."

Each witch held a crystal wine glass filled with nectar of love. To the heavens they thrust the glasses.

"The spell is now cast and true love will come to them at last. So mote it be!" The witches each drank down their love nectar in one shot.

Surrounding the altar they all smiled and nodded. The spell had worked. Matchmaking was afoot. When true love would come was up to the Goddess, but true love would indeed come to both.

FORTY SIX

"I can't believe everyone is paired off, but us." Longingly, Connie looked at the stairs knowing that her friends were tucked in with their loves.

Kandy shook her head. "It's not like we are ugly or anything. Right?"

Connie hugged her friend. "Hell no sista, we are hot stuff." She bent down picking up more wrapping paper. "Whoa, looks like we missed two presents under the tree."

Kandy knelt down and reached under the tree for two small white boxes decorated with tiny red hearts. "Hey, there is even a card."

Connie sat down next to her. "Who are they for?"

Kandy's eyes looked askance at Connie. "You are not going to believe this, but they are for us."

"For us, as in you and me?" Connie leaned over looking at the envelope. "That's weird. What does the card say."

Kandy opened the card and some small red glitter hearts fell onto the carpet, she looked down at them. "Great, more to clean." She looked back at the card and read it out loud.

"Kandy and Connie, these presents are for you and will make your love life completely new. Keep them with you to attract true love, that will fit you like a glove."

Connie looked at Kandy. "Those presents were not there before. Everyone is up getting some lovin', so how did they get there?"

"After all we've seen lately, you dare to ask." Kandy shook her head. "You keep reading and maybe we will find out who sent them."

Connie took the card from Kandy. "True love alone will not do, so sex, lust and foreplay we send to you." Connie blushed.

A red faced Kandy motioned her to go on.

"Perfect partners you will find, when it is right, when it is time. Know they exist and for you they were born, from this day, no longer mourn." Connie held out her fingers blowing on them like they were hot. "Wow!"

Kandy pulled the card from her fingers. "Believe, then see, so shall it be! It's signed the Coven of Love."

Connie handed Kandy one of the boxes. "Here goes nothing," she said ripping off the paper.

Kandy opened hers as well.

Inside each box lay two perfectly formed ruby heart shaped stones with just a smidge of white wax on them.

Kandy held hers up. "Beautiful. I can feel the energy coming from it."

Connie held hers to her chest. "I believe!" Standing up, she motioned Kandy to follow her. Once in the kitchen, she opened a cabinet and took out two wine glasses. Grabbing a bottle of red wine, she popped the cork and poured it.

Kandy took hers, lifting it up.

Connie raised her glass and touched Kandy's.

"To true love, "said Kandy.

"For both of us," said Connie.

FORTY SEVEN

She pushed him down on the bed, naked and glistening with sweat. Wearing nothing but a pair of thigh high six inch black pleather boots and the dancing ruby necklace from Lady Maveen, she reached for the bottle of Sambuca.

"Now, it is your turn to relax and enjoy, Therron. Release control to me."

Therron fought within himself. So used to being the one in charge, in life or on the job, letting her control him just wasn't something he could fathom. Yet, he trusted her like no other. "I am yours."

First one arm, then the other, she secured him to the bed using cloth restraints. Smiling, she placed restraints on both ankles and pulled his legs apart. Securing one, then the other, he lay spread eagle and at her mercy.

Standing over him, she slowly dripped Sambuca on his chest and down his abdomen.

He shuddered with each drop of the liquor. Holding the bottle in one hand, Mandy straddled him. Kneeling, she raised her butt up and licked each drop of the Sambuca with her moist tongue.

Straining to get to her neatly shaved sex box, Therron pulled each restraint in frustration.

"Easy. You will get what you want when I am ready to give it to you." She lowered herself onto his face, rubbing her fun button against his mouth. She gasped as his tongue found her center.

"That feels so good. I'm going to come if I don't stop..." Deep shudders of pleasure filled her inside and out. She lay down on him stretched out and poured Sambuca onto her hands then onto his rock hard member.

Tingles of hot pleasure shot through him as the liquor mixed with her warm mouth. Up and down she tasted him. Faster and faster, until he thought he'd die.

Suddenly she stopped and slid off him, smiling.

His breathing was heavy and shallow; he followed her with his eyes as she pulled out a box of lubricated condoms from the bedside table and slid one on his hot, ready shaft.

Holding a bottle of warming lube, she dripped it over the condom then poised her opening over him. Slowly she sunk onto him, taking his full length inside, impaling herself.

"We fit like two perfect puzzle pieces," she said locking eyes with his. Moving up and down as she rubbed her sex button on his hard abdomen, she whispered over and over, "I love you, Therron. I love you, Therron..."

His orgasm built, without him moving so much as a muscle, as his witch rode him like a wild stallion. For the first time in his life, he gave over complete control to another being whom he trusted. His witch and his alone.

Her breathing grew rapid and shallow, as tingling built within her center, then shattered outward filling her body with waves of pure pleasure. "Oh my friggin' gosh!"

He shot his load into the condom, letting waves and waves of pleasure fill his mind and body. He felt her come again and again.

Fully sated, she lay prostrate on top of him and whispered into his ear. "You rock my world, Therron Jessie Reyes - Mythos."

"And you mine, Mandy Devine." He pulled at the restraints. "Now, how about you release me so I can hold you."

She eased her body off his and stood on wobbly legs. She untied each tether slowly until his last hand was free.

He grabbed her and pulled her on top of him. "How did I get so lucky?"

"Not bad for an old lady." She winked.

"Old lady? You're younger than me by two hundred and fifty years darlin'."

"Two hundred and fifty years! You didn't tell me I was dating an old geezer!" She tickled his arm pits.

He rolled on top of her, pinning her to the mattress. "Old huh, well I guess I'm just gonna have to show you how we old ones do it." Claiming her mouth he kissed her, tickling her with his fangs.

Outside the window a raven crowed. Therron and Mandy looked at each other, faces dropping.

"It can't be that late, can it?" Therron jumped out of bed, pulling on sweat pants and a tee shirt.

Mandy pulled on her plush white and pink robe. Running her fingers through her sex mused, long hair, she followed Therron to the window.

He opened the window and in flew two ravens.

"Mom?" Therron starred at the raven with a purple bow around her thin neck.

"It is I, son! I'm so sorry I didn't have a chance to hug you again before I returned to my feathers. Alas, we were both busy weren't we?" She winked a midnight black eye at Mandy.

"Who is your little friend, Mother?" Therron starred at the other raven that looked suspiciously like a certain pilot he knew.

"Just for twenty-four hours, Therron and then you can have your Henry back. He wanted to experience what it feels like to actually fly." She gazed at the other raven with undisguised lust.

"Henry, you and I are supposed to be in the cock pit. Just how am I going to explain this one?" Therron went nose to beak with the big black bird.

"Caw a cam a sam." Henry jutted his black chest out.

Lady Raven laughed, fluffing her feathers. "He hasn't quite got the talking thing down as yet, so we have to communicate as ravens."

"Caw de mk xcuse," Henry said.

"I can even make that one out," Mandy said.

The two birds touched beaks then spread their wings to fly. Raven left first through the window calling back, "Love you son, and you too Mandy. See you tomorrow."

"Thnkssss buuddy," Henry called as he shot out behind Raven.

"They do make a striking couple," Mandy said pushing down laughter.

Therron shook his head. "A speeding witch steals my heart and my mother the raven, steals my best co-pilot."

He turned to Mandy and pulled her to his broad chest. Kissing the top of her head, he whispered, "And I wouldn't have it any other way."

HALLOWEEN THE NEXT YEAR

Shadows covered the witches, dressed in traditional black witch garb as they flew through the air on their magical brooms. Two ravens guided them as they drifted in and out of the clouds.

Circling the scene below each smiled. The ravens flapped their wings then dived. The witches followed.

Party goers screamed, dashing aside, scrambling for cover.

Kids dressed in their finest Halloween costumes pointed upwards. They scrambled, running to hide so the witches didn't eat them.

The ravens landed on top of the pool house eerily calling to each other.

Shivers ran up Frank's back. "Damn, they're good."

Therron nodded. "Almost too good. Those kids are gonna wet their pants."

The two men looked at each other and burst out laughing.

Suddenly, his witch was hovering before him. "Dare you laugh at The Witches of Raven's Hood?" Mandy winked.

Therron recoiled in pretend terror. He dropped to his knees. "Please forgive me, witch."

"I forgive you, handsome." She tapped him with her wand, and then zoomed off to join the other witches who had landed in the middle of the party.

Each year party goers paid big bucks to attend the annual Double Winker's Club Halloween Fundraiser. It was the hit of the season because they never knew what might happen. Not with real witches in the mix.

The greyhounds wandered in and out of the crowds paying no attention to the frightening scene. A piece of yummy cake here, a french fry there, all tasted good.

In a prearranged spot, a couple backed away from their teenage son who was dressed in black and had piercings covering his face.

"Does thou think you can hide from me, little boy?" Kerri Ember looked down at the angry young man.

He stomped towards her hovering broom. "You don't scare me, I know this is all just a big show." He batted his hand at her broom.

"Really?" said all the witches who were suddenly circling the teenager on their flying sticks.

"On this night of witches delight, me thinks you need a lesson of fright!" Erinna held up her wand dramatically.

"Whatever," said the punk and turned to walk away.

"Goddess, I ask you to show this boy what is true, and how his actions are affecting you." Janae

Starling looked skyward, her witch hat nearly falling from her head. Hastily she straightened it.

The wind whipped around lifting the boy up and held him hovering over the crowd. The witches charged skyward riding along side of him on their brooms.

"Hang on and enjoy the 'show'," said Arleeina. She took off, pulling the boy behind her. He flew through the air, eyes bulging out, as screaming witches surrounded him.

Higher and higher they flew, until a large cloud obscured them all from view.

A huge mirror like surface appeared beneath the teen. His future, if he continued on the path he was on, flashed before him. It wasn't pretty. Horror covered his face. "What... what is this?"

Mandy flew on his left and Kit on his right, as they all shot through the dark sky.

"That, little boy, is your life as it will be if you continue on your current path. Treating your parents like crap, not going to school, smoking pot." Kit tapped the mirror with her wand.

His eyes widened, looking at Kit with surprise. "Who the hell are you?"

"Now, is that any language to use in the presence of the most powerful witches in the world?" Mandy grabbed the mirror and flung it into the cloud. It shattered to a million pieces, along with his tough guy exterior.

He looked down at the ground far below. Dizziness assailed him and tears filled his eyes. Black eye liner ran down his face.

"Maybe we had better take the wimp down. Doesn't appear half as tough as he was on the ground," Deborah said.

"Why are you doing this to me? Where are my parents?"

"We are doing this to you so that you may have a second chance. You can change your life and what you saw as your future, will no longer be." Arleeina pointed at him with her wand. "The choice is up to you!"

"I want to change. I have for a long time, but I'm kind of stuck in this persona I've created. I wasn't well liked and I was the one being bullied before I started dressing and acting like this." He pointed to his black clothing, spiked hair and piercings.

"I can help you with the bullies, if you choose to change." Kandy Hart tapped her upper chest.

"Promise you will start believing in yourself and follow your dreams not your fears. Do better in school and give your parents no more problems from now on and I will in turn not eat you." Kerri Ember jabbed her finger at him, smiling.

He laughed for the first time since he'd taken to the sky. Tears streaming down his face, he looked each witch in the eyes. "If you will help me, guide me, I promise I will change and follow my dreams not my fears."

The witches reached out, touching their hands to the boy. His eyes opened wide with sudden fear, unsure what they were doing. "Hey, I mean it!"

"Goddess and God, we believe he will change. Help him now to rearrange. Face his fears, follow his dreams. If bullies appear, let them beware, this boy's allies will they fear. Give him strength, make him proud, speak his truth, say it loud! This we ask, this we beg, help him stand his ground on his two firm legs. So mote it be!" the witches said in unison.

The piercings dislodged from his body, falling softly to the ground. His features changed from angry fear to self-worth and determination. His black clothing fell away to reveal a witches garb. He now rode his own broom.

"Wow! This is awesome!" The boy smiled. "Thank you all!"

Mandy hovered next to him. "Do you want to go right back down to the party, or do a fly by before we land?"

The rest of the witches looked on expectantly.

"Definitely a fly by!" He held onto his broom, balancing with care.

"Oh, I love fly bys!" Kit said. She pulled out her cell phone and dialed Frank. He answered first ring. "We are requesting a fly by." She laughed and pointed at the phone.

The clouds parted below. Frank was looking up shaking his head no and waving them off.

"Ready ladies and gent?" Mandy said. She pointed below. "Let's go!"

The group of witches dove straight down towards the party goers who once more scattered. Like fierce fighter jets, the group swooped down and flew across the party goers, creating a small sonic boom.

They shot straight up, but not before they all caught a glimpse of the boy's smiling parents.

Coming around again, they landed with Mandy and Kit holding onto the boy's broom so he'd didn't crash.

He got off the broom and ran to his two parents standing with open outstretched arms.

Kit and Mandy carried their brooms inside and locked them in the closet. The other witches offered broom rides for $100.00 a fly. The fund raiser was shaping up to be the best one ever for The Double Winker's Club.

Therron and Frank followed them inside.

"Hello, beautiful," Frank said.

"Hello, handsome," Kit said as she wrapped her arms around her man's lean waist.

"Hello, my witch," said Therron.

Mandy smiled as she wrapped her arms around his neck and leaned in and whispered. "I've been a very bad witch and I need to be taught a lesson vampire." She exhaled into his ears, her warm breath sending chills up his spine.

He grabbed her hand. "Later," he said to Frank and Kit. The entwined lovers headed upstairs to Yellow Cottage.

Frank gazed down into Kit's eyes. "I'm in need of some magic myself."

Kit stood on her pointed tips and kissed him. "Last one to the bed has to make it for the next week."

"You're on..."

With a wave she disappeared.

"No fair!" He ran out the kitchen and up the stairs.

Through the sliding doors, Connie and Kandy watched the lovers disappear.

"They are so lucky." Kandy sighed.

"Someday we will be too, sista." Connie reached down to pick up a glass of punch. Her hand met up with someone else's.

"Oh, I'm so sorry," she looked up to find a handsome witch smiling at her. Still touching his hand, a sudden shyness over took the normally vivacious blonde.

He smiled back at her revealing perfect white teeth. "Ladies first." He pulled his hand out from under hers gently and picked up the punch cup, handing it to her.

"Thank you," she said.

"My name is..."

Lady Raven appeared suddenly, landing right on the stranger's shoulder.

"Connie have you met Therron's cousin, Daniel?" The raven looked from Daniel to Connie fluffing her feathers as though she had arranged this meeting. "He flew in just for the party tonight."

Connie reached out her hand and Daniel grasped it in a firm handshake. "Nice to meet you, Daniel."

Her senses felt alive for the first time in years just by standing across from the dark haired, 5'10 hunk of a witch.

Kandy coughed.

Connie turned, embarrassed that she'd forgotten her friend. "Daniel, this is my dear friend and fellow witch, Kandy Hart."

Daniel smiled. "Hello, Kandy." His eyes turned back to Connie, his intentions clear.

Lady Raven fluttered her wings then flew away. Henry flew alongside of her, in raven form for tonight.

"Well, I'll go give some more rides while you two get acquainted." Kandy backed away dragging her broom behind her.

She kicked a plastic cup, sending it in the pool. "Darn it." She dragged her broom over to the pool and set it on a chaise lounge. Kneeling down on the lip of the pool she bent forward to grab the cup.

A handsome blonde dressed in a fireman's uniform knelt beside her. "Need some help?"

Caught off guard, she lost her balance and fell towards the cold water. "Ahhh."

The fireman reached out wrapping his strong arms around her, but it was too late, and together they both went head first into the pool.

Gasps went up, as everyone from the party gathered around the pool.

Two heads popped up in the middle of the pool.

Kerri Ember and Windra Dragonfly quickly flew over top of them.

"Are you okay, Kandy?" Windra asked.

"Yeah Windra, I'm great," she said sarcastically.

The fireman burst out laughing and Kandy joined him.

"Yeah, me too," he said.

Kerri Ember and Windra smiled and then off they flew giggling.

Kicking his feet to keep afloat, he extended his hand. "Hi, I'm Kenny Jett."

Kandy treaded water. She reached out and shook his hand. "Any relation to Joan?" She giggled.

"Um, no. And you are?"

"Kandy Hart."

"Any relationship to those sweet yet tangy, candy hearts?"

She laughed water dripping from her short blonde hair. "U'm, no."

"Well, Mrs. Hart, let me get you out of this pool."

"It's Miss." She held on as he helped her over to the side of the pool, once there, she grabbed onto the side.

"Okay, Miss it is. Do you have a steady boyfriend?" He didn't get out of the pool, but looked directly into her eyes.

"You aren't very subtle are you, Kenny Jett?" Kandy splashed him with the cold water. "I'm single. How about you?"

"Single and looking." He winked. "Looking for you." He leaned in and gave her a quick kiss on her wet lips.

Looking up into the sky now filled with shining stars. "Thank you," she whispered.

Kenny smiled. "You're welcome."

She shook her head and decided that some things are just better left unexplained. She touched the small red heart she'd made into a necklace.

The witches and two ravens were poised above the party smiling down at all the love that was present.

"I just love a happy ending," said Janae.

Raven cawed and then they all flew off. Where they were heading, only they knew, but something tells me it won't be long before we find out.

The End

I hope you enjoyed the read! All good wishes!

Laura